Never in his life _____ *a smile. Warm and real and...well, sweet and saucy, too. How in heaven's name had this woman seen anything in him to pique her interest?*

Or, for that matter, sit in his living room with a smile?

Those thoughts swirled and spun. He opened his mouth, set to say something—anything.

Swallowing hard, he forced his body to move in Haley's direction before she noticed his awkwardness. Or worse, commented on his awkwardness.

Lord, he was a mess.

Rattled. Confused. Unshaven. Yup, a mess, and in that second, what he needed the most was to know what motivated Haley Foster to behave in the way she did.

"Why'd you come over here tonight, Haley?"

Dear Reader,

Every now and then a story comes along that grabs ahold of my heart and refuses to let go. This is one of those stories. I'm beyond excited to share the journey that awaits Haley Foster—the youngest sibling in the Colorado Fosters—and Gavin Daugherty, a loner of a man who is somewhat of a newcomer to Steamboat Springs, Colorado.

On the outside, these two people couldn't be more different. Haley was raised in a close-knit, loving family with three older brothers who always had her back. Gavin grew up mostly being shuttled from one foster home to another, and other than a precious few, no one has ever had his back, and his relationship with his mother is...challenging, at best. Haley follows her heart and trusts her instincts above all else, while Gavin almost always obeys the rules of logic.

They are, in most every way, oil and water. This doesn't stop Haley from listening to her gut, which insists that Gavin is meant to play an essential role in her life. And poor Gavin—he hasn't ever come face-to-face with such a feisty, impulsive woman before. He is unprepared when Haley begins to knock down every last barrier he's ever erected, and he isn't quite sure what to make of the whirlwind of contradictory emotions Haley has brought to the surface.

The road ahead of Gavin and Haley is long, twisty and filled with plenty of bumps, but if these two can stay on course, they'll find that fate has the perfect destination in store for them.

Happy Reading!

Tracy Madison

Haley's Mountain Man

—

Tracy Madison

H_{TM} **HARLEQUIN**® SPECIAL EDITION®

Recycling programs
for this product may
not exist in your area.

ISBN-13: 978-0-373-65761-2

HALEY'S MOUNTAIN MAN

Printed in U.S.A.

Books by Tracy Madison

Harlequin Special Edition

Miracle Under the Mistletoe #2154
A Match Made by Cupid #2170
An Officer, a Baby and a Bride #2195
ΔCole's Christmas Wish #2231
ΔHaley's Mountain Man #2279

*The Foster Brothers
ΔThe Colorado Fosters

Other titles by this author available in ebook format.

TRACY MADISON

lives in northwestern Ohio with her husband, four children, one bear-size dog, one loving-but-paranoid pooch and a couple of snobby cats. Her house is often hectic, noisy and filled to the brim with laugh-out-loud moments. Many of these incidents fire up her imagination to create the interesting, realistic and intrinsically funny characters that live in her stories. Tracy loves to hear from readers. You can reach her at tracy@tracymadison.com.

For many reasons, this story is dedicated to the friends who make up my extended family. You know who you are, and you know why. Thank you for your love, support and belief.

Chapter One

The lazy, hazy days of summer couldn't get here soon enough. Well, the hazy days, anyway. No one who lived in Steamboat Springs, Colorado, would describe summer as lazy. They would describe *now* as lazy. Relaxing. Maybe even rejuvenating.

Not Haley Foster. She was, in fact, bored out of her ever-living skull.

Admittedly, an odd state of being. With the hectic winter tourist season behind them and the summer season yet to arrive in full force, she *should* be enjoying the brief slowdown. She always had in the past. This year, though, she was…restless.

More than that, really. She had this itchy, uncomfortable sense of waiting for something—*anything*—to happen. What, exactly, she didn't have a clue. Just…something.

And that was why she couldn't wait for summer. The tourists would breeze in to spend their vacations white-water rafting, hiking, canoeing, or any one of the many other activities available in the area, and her sleepy town would wake again. She would be busy from sunup to sundown, and wouldn't have the time to worry about why she felt so off.

Sighing, she leaned back in her chair at the Beanery, the local coffee joint, and tried to pay attention to her longtime friend Suzette Solomon. They'd met earlier for a Saturday morning Spinning class. Now, they were supposed to be savoring their reward of yummy hot beverages while catching up on each other's lives.

Suzette was in the midst of sharing a funny story about one of her fourth-grade students, and while Haley managed to chuckle and insert a comment here and there, mostly she couldn't pull herself out of her own head long enough to relax. Dammit! She'd really believed that an hour of hard exercise followed up by a solid dose of friend time would ease the edginess.

She'd been wrong.

Why was she so freaking restless? And for that matter, why did she feel as if life were passing her by? She wasn't old, for crying out loud. At twenty-six, she had plenty of time to do anything she wanted to do. But lately, the days and the nights had seemed interminably long, and even when she was with her family or friends, she had the inexplicable sensation of…loneliness.

Maybe she needed to take up a new hobby. Or buy a pet. Or… When an epiphany failed to strike, she decided to place the full blame on being stuck between seasons. Had to be. Why search for a deeper meaning when the simplest answer was usually the culprit?

Suzette cleared her throat and watched Haley expectantly, apparently waiting for some type of a response. Oh, crap. Was this a laugh, be shocked or commiserate moment? She went with a soft chuckle, hoping that would cover all possible bases.

"Cute story, huh?" Suzette asked, ruffling her short black hair with her fingers.

"So cute," Haley agreed enthusiastically.

"Yeah? What was your favorite part?"

"Um, honestly, I don't think I can choose a favorite. The entire story was just adorable, and really, I bet cute and adorable stuff happens every single day in your classroom."

"Really, Haley?" Suzette gave her a long, semi-amused look. "You're seriously going to pretend that you didn't zone out a good five or ten minutes ago?"

Sighing again, Haley offered a faint smile. "I'm sorry. Was I that obvious?"

"Obviously, or I wouldn't have noticed." Wrapping her hand around her coffee cup, Suzette said, "No worries, though. I know I can go on and on about my students."

"I like hearing about your students!" And she did. Usually. "I was thinking about how slow the days are, and how I can't wait for summer to get here so everything can pick up again. That's all." Close enough to the truth. As close as she wanted to get, anyway.

"Since when? For almost the entire winter, all I heard was how anxious you were for enough empty hours in the day to read a book, watch a movie, paint your apartment." She arched a finely plucked eyebrow. "Go out on a few dates. Which, actually, I wanted to ask—"

"I've read the books and watched the movies I wanted to, and you helped me paint my apartment. So now, I'm ready for summer."

"Hmm, yes. But you left one item off of that list. Tell me, how many dates have you racked up in the past few months?"

Wrinkling her nose, Haley sipped her chai tea. Suzette already knew the answer to that question. "My lack of a dating life has nothing to do with my boredom." Her loneliness, maybe, but she didn't feel like broaching that topic. "I'm just bored."

"Uh-huh. Sure you are."

"You know how it is in between seasons," she argued, hoping beyond hope that she was right, and that once summer rolled in, these odd feelings would disappear. "Instead of twelve-hour workdays, I barely have enough on my agenda to stay busy for eight."

Haley's family owned two businesses in Steamboat Springs. All of the Fosters—Haley, her three older brothers, and their parents—were partners in the running of said businesses. During the winter and summer months, that meant keeping up with her normal duties as well as helping out in the restaurant and in the sporting goods store.

In the spring and fall, though, she was primarily in the office contending with the businesses' basic accounting needs, updating their websites, and ordering supplies and inventory. Most of which she'd long since mastered, so typically, none of it took very long.

"I do know how it is," Suzette agreed easily. Her parents were also local business owners, and Suzette had worked at their deli during summers until she'd graduated from college. "Your work schedule isn't the issue. Or what's really bothering you, so why don't we talk about that?"

"Stop." Forcing a laugh, she wished that Suzette didn't know her quite so well. In this particular context, anyway. "There isn't anything else bugging me."

"You're in a funk, dating-wise," Suzette said matter-of-factly, as if Haley hadn't spoken. "Happens to all of us at one time or another. But as they say, the first step is admitting an issue exists. So, I have an idea to fix your boredom and make a certain someone—"

"Stop," she repeated, sensing the conversation was headed

directly toward blind-date land. "There isn't an issue. None! And I have no desire to be fixed up with anyone."

"Even if that guy is cute, sweet and funny?"

"Even if."

"Intelligent and warmhearted?"

"Even if," she repeated. "And if he's that amazing, why aren't you dating him? Unless… Oh, no, Suzette. You're not trying to fix me up with one of your leftovers, are you?"

"One date, and not even a real date, and we didn't even kiss," she said with a flick of her wrist. "So nope, not a leftover. Promise."

"Darn close, though. Jeez."

Letting out a huff, Suzette said, "Just say the words, Haley. Dating. Funk."

"So speaks the woman who juggles three men on any given weekend." Haley was only half joking. Her friend always seemed to have a man on each arm.

"Only because I'm not as choosy as you." Narrow shoulders lifted in a slight shrug. "If a nice guy asks me out, I tend to say yes. Whereas you tend to pluck excuses from the air in order to say no." Bracing her elbows on the table, she rested her chin in her hands. "I have a better question for you. How many dates have you turned down in the past few months?"

Mentally doing the math, Haley frowned. She'd declined a handful of invitations, so what? Lonely was one thing. Dating someone she wasn't interested in was another. "I don't see the point in spending an evening with a man based on how nice he is."

"Because spending an evening with a nice guy is…such a horrible experience?"

"Not at all! He should be nice, obviously, but there should also be something more."

"Sexual attraction is always a plus, but—"

"I'm not even talking about that," Haley interrupted. Not

that she disagreed. But, "I don't want to know every detail about a man's life before we order drinks. I want to be… curious about a man, about what makes him tick."

And that right there was her real issue. Despite how *nice* many of the local men were, she just knew them too freaking well for them to hold any real interest. When you could all too easily picture a man swallowing mouthfuls of glue or picking his nose from their elementary school days, it was hard to see him in a different light. Unfair, she knew, but the truth.

Sure, she'd dated plenty in the past. None of those relationships had evolved into anything. Some of those failures she placed squarely on her big brothers' shoulders. Sweet as they were, they could also be a little *too* overprotective. The rest…well, the guys had either turned out to be jerks, or there simply hadn't been enough chemistry.

In other words, unless she moved to another city—which she had absolutely no desire to do—her future love life looked pretty darn bleak.

Maybe she should let Suzette fix her up. The thought was defeating somehow, and for whatever reason, not something she wanted to do. Yeah, she should get a pet.

A cat, maybe. Or ten. Didn't all spinsters have a houseful of cats?

"Are you saying what I think you are?" Suzette asked, her voice this side of shocked. Perhaps even a little amused. And damn if Haley could figure out where her mind had gone.

"Er, I don't know," she said. "What do you think I'm thinking?"

"Are you considering having a summer fling with a hot, hunky tourist or two?"

Laughter burbled out of Haley's throat. It felt good, even if the thought was ludicrous. "Oh, come on, that is not why I'm ready for summer. You know me better than that."

"I do, but a girl can hope. Besides, why not?"

She had nothing to say to that. Not one thing.

"It could be fun," Suzette prodded. "How will you know unless you give it a try?"

"Um, because I do. I'm not interested." Tourists weren't around long enough to appeal, and she wanted something more meaningful than a fling. Tired of trying to explain a yearning she didn't quite understand, she said, "You were right to begin with. I'm too picky."

"Look, Haley," Suzette said, her voice becoming serious, "you're thinking too hard about this! Date a few guys. Have some fun. You don't have to marry any of them, but it has to better than sitting at home wishing for twelve-hour workdays. Which is rather nuts, you know."

"I know, but—"

The door flew open and a man entered. Blinking, she watched him stride toward Lola, the owner of the Beanery and, as it so happened, a close friend of Haley's mother. He held a clipboard in one hand, the other was squeezed into a fist at his side, and every ounce of his body seemed intense and...hard, as if he were prepared for a fight.

She had drawn the same impression when she'd originally met him, back in December. His name was Gavin Daugherty, and he was somewhat of a newcomer to Steamboat Springs. At the time, he'd come into the sports store looking for work as a ski instructor. They hadn't had any positions available, but her brother Cole had latched onto her interest—*curiosity*—and for a while, had seemed bent on finding out more about Gavin.

Fortunately, Cole's attention had become otherwise occupied by his now-fiancée, Rachel Merriday, and he'd seemingly forgotten all about Gavin.

But Haley hadn't. The man had been on her mind a lot.

Silly, really, as she knew hardly anything about him, and had seen him only a few times since. Curious, she watched as he got into line behind four others to wait his turn. The woman in front of him instantly stepped forward, putting a few more inches of space in between her and him. Gavin stepped forward as well, as folks were apt to do when a line moved. The woman attempted to move up again, but she didn't have any room left to do so.

Instead, she sidled to the side. Without missing a beat, Gavin retreated a few inches and gestured for the woman to retake her place in line. She didn't look at him and, rather than moving closer, she stepped another few inches in the opposite direction, and then several more.

A slow burn began inside as Haley put two and two together. She had a sense that people backed away from Gavin often. She supposed that was due in part to his size, as he was a giant of a man. Probably around six-foot-five, he had the build of a linebacker that only began with the wide, muscular breadth of his shoulders. And okay, he could use a haircut and a shave to get rid of the Grizzly Adams look he had going. Even so, his appearance didn't scare her or make her uneasy. She could see, however, how others might view him as intimidating.

"So what do you say?" Suzette asked, interrupting her thoughts. "Can't be next weekend, but if I can put something together for the weekend after next, are you game? Please say yes."

"Um, sure," Haley said, entirely focused on Gavin. "Whatever, whenever, is fine."

"That's great! We'll have fun, you'll see. And I know you'll like Matt."

"Uh, what?" Returning her attention to her friend, Haley said, "Wait a minute. Who is Matt and why does it matter if I'll like him or not?"

"Matt is the guy we've been talking about. He's one of the

teachers I work with." Suzette smiled smugly and crossed her arms over her chest. "And you just agreed to a double date."

"No way, Suzette." Haley shook her head to back up her words. "I'm not interested in a blind date, double or otherwise."

"You already agreed," Suzette said in a singsong voice. "So, tough. I swear, he's a great guy. And since he didn't grow up here, you can learn all about what makes him tick. That is what you said you wanted, right?"

Scowling, she pushed a strand of hair off her cheek. "It is, but you're being unfair. I didn't know what I was agreeing to." Unable to stop herself, Haley turned to look at Gavin again.

"Yep, but whose fault is that?"

"Mine, but you took advantage."

"True. I'm holding you to it, though. For your own sake." Following the direction of Haley's gaze, she asked, "What is so interesting up there that you can't stop staring?"

Letting the topic drop—for now—Haley asked, "Do you see that guy?"

"Mr. Mountain Man? Yeah, he's hard to miss."

"If you were standing in line with him, would you feel uncomfortable or...threatened?"

Suzette shrugged. "I might, if he looked at me funny. He's a big guy and look at how he's standing—all stiff and straight, like he's rearing up to pounce or something. If he just stood there and ignored me, though, I wouldn't give him a second thought. Why ask for trouble, right?"

"Exactly."

"He has a killer body, though," Suzette mused. "I wonder if he's hot beneath all that hair. Do you know him?"

"Not really." Quickly draining the rest of her tea, she stood. "I'm going to get another. Do you want anything?"

"Ah...no. I think I'm good." Suzette glanced from Haley to

Gavin and back again. "Him? You're interested in that guy? He doesn't look to be your type."

Heat suffused Haley's cheeks. "I want more tea, Suzette. That's all. And how do you know what my type is, anyway? I don't even know what my type is."

Suzette regarded her silently for a few seconds before donning a bright smile. "I know that Matt is your type, and I know you'll enjoy meeting him."

"I'm… Oh. The hell with it. Fine, I'll go." Simpler to agree than to continue to argue a case she wouldn't win. Besides which, she was allergic to cats. "One time only. End of discussion."

"For now, but you might change your mind after meeting Matt." Twisting her wrist to look at her watch, she made a face. "I have to run. Plans tonight and a lot to do beforehand."

"You can't stay for a little longer?"

"I'm sorry, I can't. Even if I could, I'm not up to feeling like a third wheel." Standing, Suzette gave her a quick hug. "It probably won't be this week, because Matt's heading home to see his family for a few days, but once I have the details set for our double date, I'll call."

"Yay," Haley said with zero enthusiasm. "Can't wait."

"Okay, I have to run." She gave one more question-filled glance toward Gavin before saying, "Just…ah…be careful. With your *tea*."

Haley opened her mouth to argue—again—but snapped it shut. There was something to be said about protesting too much. Rather, she simply smiled and waved goodbye. Once Suzette had exited the Beanery, she expelled a breath and smoothed her shirt. Resisted the impulse to do the same with her hair, and pushed herself forward…toward the mountain man.

Just out of curiosity's sake, she assured herself. Nothing more than that. Because Suzette had been right on the money—Gavin Daugherty was not her type. He was, in fact, the physical opposite of every man she had ever dated. Taller, bigger, gruffer.

He intrigued her, though, which was something a man hadn't done in a long, long while. The thought was…compelling.

Almost irresistibly so.

Chapter Two

Crowds in general made Gavin Daugherty uneasy. Being around too many folks at once brought on a plethora of miserable sensations. Out of nowhere, his throat would grow scratchy and dry, his palms would sweat and even the collar of his shirt went on attack, tightening incrementally around his neck until he found a way to get the hell out of dodge.

Exactly the reasons he'd chosen midmorning to arrive at the Beanery. He'd hoped to hit the sweet spot and find the place near empty. Rather, it being a Saturday and all—a fact he should've considered—the coffee shop was teeming with people. When he first walked in, he'd had half a mind to turn around and try for better luck on Monday.

Truth was, though, he'd already waited too damn long. He should have been on top of this months ago. So, like it or not—and he didn't—here he was, waiting in the slowest-moving line on earth to speak with Lola, mentally rehearsing the speech he'd spent the past several weeks preparing, and trying not to spook the lady to the front and right of him again.

Asking anyone for anything was about as far out of Gavin's comfort range as standing in the middle of the busy coffee shop, but he had to do it. If he had any hope of his plan succeeding, he couldn't sit back and wait for his entire lousy life to do a one-eighty without putting forth any effort. The thought had no more crossed his mind before he changed it. Much of his life had hit below the lousy line, but not all of it. Not by a long shot.

Now…well, now was fairly decent. And he couldn't forget Russ and Elaine Demko or the gifts they'd given him, either. God, he hated thinking that both of them were gone.

Little had his scruffy, twelve-year-old self known how fortunate he was to be placed with them, or how much he would come to love them. Yep, he'd been headed down the wrong path at full speed when Russ and Elaine became his foster parents, and damn if he knew how, but they'd seen clear through his tough act and shown him what family, and being a part of one, meant.

He'd stayed with them only for a little over two years before they'd decided to move out of state. Work-related, he'd been told. They hadn't forgotten him, though, and had kept in touch on holidays and his birthday and a letter here and there. It had hurt, sure, but he'd found some peace in knowing they cared, that they were out there somewhere, still caring.

Elaine had died several years back, from cancer. Russ just about two years ago now, from a heart attack. Or, more likely, heartbreak. And he'd gone and left Gavin some money. Not a little and not a lot, but some. Enough to buy some land. Enough to situate himself, to get started here, in Steamboat Springs, where Russ and Elaine had brought Gavin a time or two while he'd lived with them. Good days. Good memories.

He'd rather have Russ and Elaine.

Gavin stifled a sigh tinged with sadness and relief when the damn line finally moved forward by one. Lola, she liked to chat up her customers, that was for sure. Good business sense combined with a naturally friendly nature, he supposed.

Before stepping forward, he darted a glance toward the right, curious if enough space now existed for the woman to retake her place in front of him. That would be a…no. She inched herself up but maintained her hovering-to-the-side position as if her very life depended on it.

Accustomed to the behavior or not, it rankled.

His clothes were clean and well kept, if not brand-spanking-new. *He* was clean and…well, relatively well kept, though a shave probably wouldn't be out of order. He hadn't said a word to the woman, for crying out loud. So yes, it disturbed him, the way folks stepped out of his path when they saw him coming or refused to look him in the eye. And when little old ladies clutched their purses to their chests and watched him in a mix of distrust and fear, he just about died inside. He was used to it, but he wanted more.

Stupid to think Steamboat Springs, Colorado, would be any different. It wasn't. Folks here treated him the same as they did anywhere else, except for a handful of them. Lola being one, which was why he'd decided to start with her. He wasn't about to give up.

Someday, he'd walk these streets and folks would raise their hands and say hi. Someday, he'd have a place here. Not just for him, but for boys stuck in the system, as he had once been. A sanctuary, albeit a temporary one, where he hoped to make some type of a difference for these kids. Just as Russ and Elaine had done for him.

That was his goal: to open a camp of sorts, for boys who didn't have real homes, where they'd learn to ski, go on hikes, sit outside around a campfire. Somehow, and he wasn't quite sure how, he wanted to show these kids what Russ and Elaine had taught him—that life kept moving, changing, morphing from one thing to another. Bad now didn't mean bad later. And he couldn't figure a better way than sharing his love of the outdoors.

Being outside, whether working or playing, had often helped Gavin feel that he was a part of something bigger, better, than whatever was going on in that moment. He'd like to pass that feeling—belief—on, if he could. And no, he didn't have all the details or specifics worked out, but he would. In time.

That was the promise he'd made to himself when he'd received the check from Russ's estate, when he'd read the letter Russ had written to him.

Turned out, the Demkos had wanted to adopt him, along with the other boy who'd been staying with them, and had actually tried to sort through the red tape before Russ's job had taken them to Massachusetts. Bad luck that they'd run out of time before they'd run out of red tape, forcing them to give up. Bad luck, as well, that Gavin's mother had chosen that exact moment to get her act together long enough to go for another chance at raising her son.

A chance she'd ruined within months. She'd had more chances, later, down the road. All of which had amounted to a big, fat pile of nothing. Just like always.

But that letter from Russ—the sheer fact of knowing that the Demkos had wanted him as their legal son—had arrived in the nick of the time. Gavin had been in Aspen, fighting with himself over a decision. And that letter… Well, Russ's words had once again altered his view of himself, of what he wanted out of life, and had pulled him off the disastrous path he'd come too close to taking. So yeah, he owed Russ and Elaine. Owed them the best he could give.

More than that, he owed himself.

Lost in the past as he was, in his hopes for the future,

Gavin didn't realize when someone else stepped into line behind him. It was the voice that filtered into his thoughts. A female voice, warm and sultry, and somehow effervescent, that broke his concentration. For a beat, he stood there and soaked in that voice, let it seep into his soul and calm his ragged emotions.

"Excuse me, ma'am?" the female said again, louder this time, more insistent. He half turned to see who was speaking and to whom, because while he'd been mistaken for many things, not a one of them had ever been a "ma'am." Thank God for that.

Ah. Haley Foster. The sweetheart of Steamboat Springs, live and in person. He knew who she was, of course, from the sporting goods store he'd tried to get a job at, but also by reputation. In this town, the Fosters were well liked, well respected and very much involved in…well, it seemed like just about everything. And while he didn't know for sure, he thought Haley was the baby of the family. Her brothers, from the few times Gavin had seen them, appeared to be older.

But who knew? He'd never been that great at guessing age. If he were to take a stab, though, he'd put her on the lower end of the twenties. Maybe midtwenties, but surely no older.

Something inside sort of tightened as he appraised her. Her long, auburn hair was up in one of those contraptions only females knew how to use, forming a loose knot that wasn't completely doing the job it was meant for. Escaped tendrils framed her face in a messy yet no less appealing sort of way. Her eyes, a riveting combination of smoke and willow and fog—green but not all-the-way green—were aimed at the woman he'd somehow spooked.

"Ma'am," she repeated. "Are you in line or…?"

The woman, apparently catching on that she was being spoken to, tilted her chin in Haley's direction. "Yes," she said. "Of course I'm in line."

Haley widened those riveting eyes of hers in a darn good imitation of surprise. "Oh. Um, you do realize that you're not actually standing in line, though. Right? I mean, I thought you were just looking at the menu, the way you're so far off to the side like that."

"I'm in line," the woman repeated. "Sorry for your confusion."

"Confusion?" Shaking her head, Haley gave the distance between the woman and Gavin and assessing glance. "Nope, not confused. In fact, I would say you're a good foot or so off from actually being *in* the line. Maybe more." She nudged—*nudged*—Gavin's arm. "Wouldn't you say that's about a foot? More or less?"

And damn if he didn't have to work hard not to laugh out loud at the woman's expression. "Easily a foot. More or less," he confirmed.

Without another word, the woman eased herself into line. And Haley…well, she winked at him, and muttered something about ignorance he couldn't quite make out under her breath.

He knew it was dumb. He knew it didn't mean a damned thing. But the fact was, the sweetheart of Steamboat Springs, Colorado, had just done something only two other people in his life had ever before done. She'd stood up for him. And that made her different.

What was that word Russ would use to describe Elaine? *Gumption.* That was it. "Boy," he'd say, usually after Elaine had rightly torn into his hide about one thing or the other, "that woman's got gumption, and a woman with gumption is a helluva lot more important ten, twenty, thirty years down the road than anything else she might have once had. Remember that."

And yep, he'd remembered. Now, looking at Miss Haley Foster and the spunky, satisfied grin she wore, it was easy to see that she was damn near overflowing with the stuff, with *gumption.* Before he went and said something to that effect, or something equally ridiculous, he gave her a quick nod and faced front again.

Not being able to see her didn't wipe the look of her out of his head, though. He felt her, too, in every ounce of his body, deeper than bone. Not so different, really, than the warmth of the sun saturating into his skin. Natural. Life-affirming. Real.

He let those words tumble around for all of thirty seconds before booting them out. She was a woman he didn't know—not really—and she didn't know him. So nope, she hadn't stood up for him, she'd asked a damn question. That was all. And comparing her physical presence to the friggin' sun? Where had that idiotic thought come from, anyway?

Didn't matter. None of it.

What *did* matter was obtaining Lola's assistance. Gavin returned his focus to that and started mentally rehearsing his speech again, all the while pretending that the warm buzz cascading over him, through him, had nothing to do with the female standing behind him.

Not one damn thing.

Gavin's flannel-shirt-covered back, every long and broad muscular inch of it, was so still, Haley couldn't determine if the man was even breathing. Disappointment, sharp and strong, cut into the anticipation that had been fizzing and popping in her blood. What had she thought would happen? That they'd strike up a conversation because she'd confronted the standoffish woman?

Yes, actually, that was what she had thought.

She chewed on her bottom lip as she stared at that long, broad back. Considered tapping his arm and just start talking. Ask him a question. Mention how nice the day was, how it was slowly warming up outside. Find out if he was a coffee or a tea drinker, or... Okay. Something less boring. Something less…predictable. Maybe she should just faint dead away at his feet and hope he'd pick her up and carry her off to wherever he lived and…and…have his way with her?

Really? She shook her head, tried to erase the image, but the darn thing refused to vanish. Warmth flooded her cheeks and dripped down her neck. A tight ball of heat gathered in her stomach, low and heavy and almost throbbing in its intensity, reminding her of how long it had been since she'd last experienced that particular sensation.

Desire. Longing. The need to be touched.

And wow, wasn't it just awesome that she'd have this experience now, here in the middle of the freaking coffee shop, over a man she barely knew, after the briefest, most innocent of encounters? Pitiful. Embarrassing. Maybe even a little sad.

But also…interesting? Yes, that, too.

The line moved again while she pondered, considering the complexities *and* the simplicities of the signals her body seemed hell-bent on sending her way. A chemical response, surely, since she didn't know Gavin. She didn't know where he came from, what his goals were, what his favorite foods were. She knew he skied, considered himself able to teach others how to ski. She knew he'd moved into the area sometime before December.

And that was the sum of her knowledge.

So, okay. A chemical response. Nothing more, nothing less. Her eyes traveled the length of him, from his untucked charcoal flannel shirt, to his denim-covered legs, to his heavy leather hiking boots. Easy to see all were clean. Well-worn, too. The jeans, the shirt, they fit his body as if he'd been wearing them, had worked and played in them, for so long that they'd formed to his shape. No other man would be able to wear those jeans and that shirt quite so well.

She looked up and up, and up some more. His hair was straight, except for the slight wave at the ends, and fell a few inches below his collar. Either he'd put off going to the barber or he was in that awkward growing-out stage. Probably the former. She tried to determine the accurate word for the color of his hair. *Brown* did the job, she supposed, but it wasn't nearly enough. In her mind, brown in and of itself was a flat, drab shade, holding little depth, little light, little of interest. But Gavin's hair was filled with light. It was thick and lustrous, rich with hues of chestnut and coffee, chocolate and cinnamon, and the odd golden strand here and there.

So, no. *Brown* didn't begin to cut it.

Beautiful, maybe. And she couldn't stop herself from wondering if that straight line of beautiful hair was as soft to the touch as it looked.

Sad and pitiful, for sure, to be gawking at a stranger's hair and wishing she could touch it. Haley shook her head and forcibly pulled herself out of her inane thoughts. Maybe Suzette had been right all along. Maybe a date with Matt the teacher was exactly what she needed.

The line moved again, and the standoffish woman gave her order. For whatever reason, Lola didn't drop into her normal banter, just asked what type of milk the woman wanted and prepared the cappuccino. The woman accepted her coffee, paid and stepped away quickly, without so much as a glance in either Gavin's or Haley's direction.

And that also struck Haley as sad. Why, though, she couldn't say.

Gavin approached the counter, stopped and turned to face Haley again. This time, she noticed his eyes. Good Lord, the man had a gorgeous set of peepers. Again, she had to search for the right description. They were gray, except they weren't. And they were blue, except not really that, either. She sighed. Mostly gray with the barest hint of blue. If a name for that exact color, in that precisely right combination of gray and blue existed, she didn't know what it was.

Beautiful would have to suffice there, as well.

"Your turn," she said, trying desperately to stop staring into his eyes.

"Actually," he said in a low drawl that made her skin tingle, her pulse hum, "you should go first. I might be a few minutes. Need to talk with Lola about a… Well, you should go first."

"No, no. I'm fine." If she went first, she'd have to walk away, and she wasn't quite ready to walk away. "You're ahead of me. That's the way lines work."

He squinted his eyes, looked as if he were going to argue, but in the end just shrugged his shoulders and nodded. Faced front again, and set the clipboard on the counter. When he spoke, it was in that deep rumble, so low she had to block out every other sound in order to hear him.

"I'll take one of those hazelnut lattes, large," he said. "And I was hoping you might have the time to hear me out on something. If not now, I can wait. Or come back another day."

"How long you needing?" Lola asked, her tone friendly and curious.

"Not long. Shouldn't need much, I don't think."

Nodding, Lola went to the espresso machine, saying, "Go on, then. I'm listening."

"Right. Okay." His spine straightened another fraction and he released a breath. "Well, I'm not sure if you knew this, but for the past year, more really, even before officially moving here, I've been working real hard on learning the area and getting all the required licenses. So I can guide folks on hikes and white-water rafting trips, and maybe some climbing—" He paused, drew in another breath. "I have everything in order now. For the summer season, and winter, too, for next season. Skiing and such."

"That's an accomplishment, all right," Lola said. "Good for you."

"Thank you. So now that I have all the paperwork set, I'm

in need of customers, and I don't really know a lot of the locals yet. Which is why I'm here. I thought I'd check in with
you, maybe see if you would be interested in—"

"Me?" Lola inserted with a chuckle. "If I had even a quar-
ter of a mind to go white-water rafting or hiking, I'm sure
you'd make an excellent guide. Truth of the matter is, those
days are about a decade behind me." Still chuckling, she
steamed the milk while the machine pumped out a double
shot of espresso. "Sweet, though, you'd think to ask, and I
appreciate it."

"Ah... Well, see. I didn't mean it exactly in that fashion,
but I don't believe you're ever too...or rather, that it's ever too
late to enjoy nature," he said, stumbling around his words.
"But that wasn't what I wanted to talk to you about."

It was, Haley decided, very cute. Sweet, even, both his
nerves and his earnestness.

Lola grabbed a bottle from the rack of flavored syrups and
gestured for him to continue.

"It's like this," he said with a small cough. "I made up
some...flyers, I'd guess you'd call them, and I was wondering if you might keep some here. Maybe put in a good word
for me. In case any of your customers ask about guides or
want some pointers or..." He trailed off, pushed the clipboard
toward Lola's side of the counter. "I guess that's about it."

Gavin's entire body tensed as he waited for Lola's reply,
and that, along with the thread of hope she'd heard in his
voice, softened her heart into a pile of goo. This mattered to
him. And for some reason she didn't have the answer for, it
suddenly mattered to her, too. She shifted to the left, just a
tad, and craned her neck to get a better view of the clipboard.

And when she saw the pages clipped there, her gooey heart
sank straight to her toes. Oh, dear. While there wasn't anything acutely wrong with the flyers Gavin had made, they
were...basic at best. His name, the services he offered and

contact information. Everything was spelled correctly, everything was easy to read. But there also wasn't anything there, in her mind at least, that would propel a would-be customer to choose Gavin's services over the multitude of others available in the area. And there were many, many such companies.

Her family's sporting goods store, for one.

Lola finished preparing Gavin's coffee, returned to the counter and, after handing him his cup, picked up the clipboard. Now, Haley tensed, waiting and hoping right along with Gavin. Lola wouldn't say no to such a simple request, would she?

"Your white-water rafting certifications include both the Colorado and the Eagle Rivers?" Lola asked in an easy, conversational tone. "And I take it you're more than passing familiar with Fish Creek Falls and Rabbit Ears Peak, feel comfortable with the trails?"

"Yes, to all of it," Gavin said. "Fully state-certified."

"Hmm. You going to start taking folks up in hot-air balloons, too?"

"What? Um." Leaning over the counter, Gavin looked at the clipboard, as if thinking that something about hot-air balloon rides had suddenly materialized. "No. Just the hikes and the rafting right now. Maybe climbing, some camping if the interest is there. But I don't know anything about hot-air balloons, haven't ever been in a hot—"

"I'm teasing," Lola said with a boisterous laugh. "And I haven't been up in one, either."

"Teasing." He sort of wagged his head as if the idea of that was beyond him. Also cute and sweet. Sad, too. "Right."

"What about referrals? And equipment? I mean, don't get me wrong, I'm happy enough to pass on your information, but folks are likely to ask." Lola gave him a measured look. "And when they do, it would be good if I could answer."

Without considering the whys, Haley threw herself forward. "Gavin is getting his equipment from us, Lola. From the store. We've worked out sort of a…partnership. And you can use my name as a referral. All of us Fosters, actually. We've all been working with Gavin, you see, helping him settle in and, well, he's an excellent guide. Just excellent."

"Is that so? I'm surprised your mother didn't mention anything." The corners of Lola's lips twitched, and Haley figured she knew the real reason Margaret Foster hadn't mentioned this partnership with Gavin Daugherty. Because one didn't exist. *Yet.* "I'm also surprised you didn't add that bit of information on these flyers, here, Gavin. Might want to—"

"That's my fault!" Again without thought, Haley grabbed the clipboard, holding it tight to her chest. "I was supposed to get the flyers and brochures and his website and everything prepared, but I spaced out. Gavin was getting everything moving along." Now she turned toward Gavin. "I'm really sorry I've been so slow. Give me another week, tops."

Eyes narrowed in speculation, Gavin reached for the clipboard. Haley clutched it tighter and eased her entire body backward. Something akin to surprise filtered into his gaze. "I… No apology necessary, Miss Foster. I am perfectly capable of handling this aspect of our…partnership without your assistance. If I could have my clipboard, please?"

"No. I insist. Really! Besides which, it would help to keep this. For reference, as I'm working on the new copy." Lola, she saw, was watching them with a fair amount of amused curiosity. Great. She'd probably be on the phone to Haley's mother within the hour. She thrust her mug toward her, saying, "I would love another chai tea. Please?"

Lola squinted her eyes but nodded. The second she turned away, Gavin whispered, "What are you doing?"

"Trying to help." Oh, dear Lord, what had she gotten herself into? Cole was surely going to kill her when she tried to convince him to go along with a plan she'd barely conceived of. Still, she wasn't prepared to back down just yet. "I can help. If you'll let me."

He worked his jaw, the muscles clenching and unclenching as he looked at her. "Why?"

"Because I want to."

"Why?"

"Because I want to," she repeated. "Nothing more, nothing less."

His entire expression hardened in disbelief. "People don't generally offer to help a stranger for no cause. Not without wanting something in return."

"I am. I want nothing, and in case you haven't noticed, I am a person, so I'd say you're wrong on that front." Why was she arguing this? If he wasn't inclined to accept her offer, she should let the matter drop. But just like the woman she had to confront, Haley couldn't—wouldn't—let this drop. "Just say yes."

A shot of blue slid into the gray of his eyes, changing them into yet another color she couldn't name. With a quick shake of his head, he held out his hand. "My clipboard. Please."

She debated refusing, but really, hadn't she made enough of a fool out of herself? Before handing it over, she ripped off the topmost page, which she then shoved into her purse.

"Sometimes," she said, "people just want to help for the sake of helping. If you change your mind, you can usually find me at Foster's Pub and Grill. I mostly work in the back, in the office, so if you don't see me, just ask for Haley."

"I won't change my mind." He closed his eyes for a millisecond, muttered under his breath. "I don't mean to be rude, but I don't know you. I prefer to tend to my own business."

She nodded, held her shoulders straight. "Okay. The offer stands."

After another long, steady appraisal, he said, "You're something, Miss Haley Foster. Definitely something." He pulled two fives out of his pocket and placed them on the counter. To Lola, he said, "For mine and hers. And I thank you for your time."

And with that, the mountain man all but marched out of the Beanery, still appearing to be a man very much prepared for a fight. When was she going to learn? She had a habit of doing this, of sticking her foot in where it didn't belong, where it wasn't wanted.

"Gee, that didn't go well," Haley murmured, accepting the tea from Lola.

"I know what you were doing, and it was sweet of you, but this man…he's got all sorts of rough edges, kiddo. And I'd estimate that he's not accustomed to sweetness." Lola patted her hand and offered a smile. "Very sweet of you, though."

"You weren't fooled for a second, were you?"

"Your mom pretty much spills all there is to spill about you kids, so no, not fooled."

"I tried, I guess." Another thought occurred to her. "Can you not mention this to my mother? Or anyone else? Um, specifically anyone with the last name Foster?"

"I suppose I can do that." Lola chuckled. "None of this is my business, now is it?"

"Thanks, Lola."

The line was lengthening again, so Haley returned to the table she'd shared with Suzette. Rough edges? Not accustomed to sweetness? She knew Lola hadn't meant to spur her forward with those two comments, but dammit, how could she *not* try harder?

Chemical response notwithstanding, she liked Gavin Daugherty. Maybe in spite of his rough edges, maybe because of them. She didn't know, and frankly, didn't altogether care at the moment. She *liked* him. And her heart was still a pile of goo.

Sighing, Haley retrieved the flyer from her purse and

stared at it, thought about how she should back off and listen to her head for once, and not her heart. That would be the smart thing to do, the practical thing to do. That would be what her brothers would insist she do.

Unfortunately, she mostly ignored her brothers when they *insisted* she do anything. And listening to her head over her heart? Paying attention to boring old logic instead of her gut? No. She wasn't very good at those, either. So, really. Why would she start now?

After another minute's consideration, she decided there were plenty of valid reasons to follow the path of logic, to think instead of feel. But she wasn't going to.

Logic be damned.

She looked through the window, considered her options, and without another second of hesitation, thrust her arms into her jacket and beelined it toward the door. If she were lucky, she'd be able to catch up to Gavin before he handed out any of those flyers.

After that… Well, she guessed she'd just play it by ear.

Chapter Three

Mind circling with questions, Gavin strode toward his battered pickup truck, berating himself for almost giving in. For that mere second of belief that someone who didn't know him would actually want to help. He knew better, but dammit, that second of belief had felt good.

More than that. It had felt...possible.

Asinine, that. Why would Haley Foster want to help him, a man she didn't know, a man who wanted to start a business that could very well cut into some of her family's income? Didn't make a lick of sense, and anything that held zero logic raised every one of his red flags.

In his truck, he tossed the clipboard on the passenger seat and slammed the door shut. Dammit. He'd been in such an all-fire hurry to leave that he hadn't left any of the flyers with Lola. So he'd have to go back, but not now. Likely not until he'd found the words to explain that there wasn't a partnership with the Fosters, that there hadn't been one to begin with and that no, he had no idea why Haley had claimed otherwise.

Closing his eyes, he rested his head against his seat and exhaled a deep breath, tried to decide his next step. He could stop in at other businesses, as he'd originally planned, but he didn't feel all that optimistic at the moment. Better to wait until he'd regrouped. Monday, maybe.

Until then, he'd put in some physical labor around his property. Spend the day outside, in the sun, working his muscles until they ached. Yeah. That should do the trick. Of course, if he didn't start earning more cash than his job at the hardware store gave him, his progress would come to a screeching halt. Not yet, though. He had a little extra left to work with, and plenty he could do with the materials he'd already purchased. Besides, however long it took, it took.

There wasn't any hurry. So long as he could move forward, he didn't rightly care how slow that motion was. He opened his eyes and shoved the key into the ignition, started the engine. Home. Work. When the day ended, he'd have put himself back to rights.

And he'd quit thinking about Haley Foster, her nonsensical offer to help and the way her almost-but-not-quite green eyes had stared into his as if she *knew* him. Shouldn't be that difficult. She was, after all, just a woman. Not much more than a girl, really. And even if her offer had somehow been up front and honest, he'd meant what he said: he preferred to tend to his own business. Especially when the business in question meant so much.

The Demkos were an aberration in a world of folks who were more concerned for themselves than anyone else. No reason to believe Haley Foster was also an aberration.

With a muffled curse, he shifted into Drive and pulled onto the road. Too much to hope for, maybe, but that didn't stop him from doing just that. The sensation was uncomfortable and threatening and dammit, he didn't like it one bit.

Reaching over, he switched on the radio and raised the volume loud enough to block out his thoughts, a maneuver that typically proved successful. Not today, and by the time he arrived home, he'd swept straight past uncomfortable into spitting mad and raring for a fight.

Well, he'd work that out, too.

And he would've, no doubt. But not thirty seconds after exiting his truck, a sky-blue compact car pulled in behind him, and the woman at the wheel was none other than Miss Haley Foster herself. She'd followed him home? Who did that?

Forget gumption. The woman was insane, and had zero sense of self-preservation. Hell, as far she knew, he was an ax murderer. Why would she put herself at risk?

He raked his fingers through his hair, silently counted to ten to rein in his irritation, his concern for her that also made no sense. Whatever she was up to, it stopped now. Had to.

Otherwise, he might go and do something stupid. He might just let that hope take root. Or…he might start believing that the rules of the world—*his* world—had somehow changed. That, he knew, would be a false belief, and when everything righted itself again—which it absolutely would—he'd be worse off.

He couldn't go there. Wouldn't let himself go there. Drawing in a deep breath, he marched forward. One way or another, this stopped now.

Perhaps if she hadn't grown up with three older brothers, Haley would've been fooled by Gavin's nod of greeting and his easy, almost loose gait as he approached. Thanks to Reid, Dylan and Cole, however, she recognized when barely restrained anger darkened a man's gaze.

So, okay. Chasing after him probably hadn't been her

smartest move. Better, less intense, if she'd used the phone number on the flyer she'd snagged. Given him the chance to get to know her a little before barging into his life uninvited. But she hadn't been thinking. She'd reacted.

She was here now, though, and she intended to have her say. Then, if he asked—or by the looks of him, ordered—her to leave, she would. Probably. No, she would. Absolutely.

Inhaling a fortifying breath, she unbuckled her seat belt and stepped from the car with her smile in place. Adrenaline pummeled through her, every bit as potent as if she'd downed an entire bottle of caffeine pills with an extra-large cola, and her heart knocked against her breastbone in a too-fast beat. Out of nerves, she told herself. Out of the belief that this—and the man himself—was important, and that she couldn't screw this up.

He came toward her, his expression serious, his eyes shadowed. Stopped in front of her and appraised her, gave his head that same slow shake she'd seen earlier. "Haley," he said, his voice gruff and low. "This is…unexpected. Why are you here?"

The way he stood and stared, waiting quietly, raised her nerves another notch. Too bad she hadn't considered exactly how to go about this, exactly how to explain her instinctual need to follow him. Instead, she grabbed on to the first words that popped into her head, lame as they were, and said, "You ran out of the Beanery so fast, I didn't have the chance to thank you."

He blinked. "Thank me?"

"For the tea. And I wanted to thank you. So, um, thanks!"

Creases lined his forehead and his jaw did that clenching, unclenching thing again, and she knew—just knew—he was still working hard to keep his anger at bay. "Are you in some type of trouble that I should know about?"

"Nope. No trouble."

"There isn't a crazed boyfriend hot on your heels you need protecting from?"

"Nope," she repeated, weirdly pleased by this question. She might have taken the opportunity to flirt—just a little—but a chunk of long, loose hair fell into her face. She brushed it aside. "Don't have any boyfriend at the moment, let alone a crazed one."

Disbelief coated his expression, and that pleased her, too.

"Your car isn't making funny noises that have you concerned?" he asked in an even, almost rigid manner. "You're not ill or injured or in need of any medical attention whatsoever?"

"Car is running great.… Well, maybe not great, but certainly nothing out of the ordinary, and I'm feeling terrific. Really…terrific. I do, however, appreciate your concern." She widened her smile, batted her eyelashes. "Greatly, even. Very sweet of you to ask."

"That's me all right, sweet." He pushed out a short breath. "And I'm guessing you're not here to borrow a cup of sugar or to sell me something, correct?"

"Correct! I'm all set in the sugar department. And, I don't know. Are you looking to buy anything?" Uh-oh. Based on the scowl currently decorating the mountain man's face, she might have gone a little too far to the flippant side of the equation. "Listen, I really just wanted—"

"Glad you're all set. Hope you enjoyed the drive here, and take care on the drive back." With those tersely uttered words, he pivoted and strode in the direction of his truck, his gait no longer easy or loose. Just…bam, he'd heard enough and was done with the conversation.

Unaccustomed to people walking away from her, Haley sucked in a surprised breath. What should she do? Chase after him again, or get in her car and drive away, as he wanted her to? She could almost hear every one of her brothers' voices chiming in that she should leave. *Now.* Before she did something she might regret.

Only problem was she didn't want to leave. If anything, the very fact that Gavin had asked after her well-being when faced with such a peculiar situation spoke volumes. Showed her the strength of his character, she supposed. Maybe even proved her instincts were right all along, which really, she hadn't doubted. Much.

He was mad. No doubt about it. Frustrated, too, probably. But he'd tempered both emotions and chose, instead, to ascertain that she didn't require any assistance. Yes, she liked him.

The tight ball of heat returned in her lower stomach, just as intense, just as real as before, shocking her with its strength. Okay, *liked* was an understatement. A sigh born from her own frustration slipped from her lips. Nope, she wasn't leaving. Couldn't, really.

There had to be a way to get through to him.

"Wait!" she hollered. He didn't pause, didn't look over his shoulder, just kept on walking in the opposite direction. Feeling very much like a lost puppy—or maybe even a stalker, at least from his perspective—she set off at a half jog on wobbly, Jell-O-filled legs. "Please? I only want a few minutes to talk. I'll leave then. Promise."

Whether it was due to the *please* or the *promise,* she didn't know, but he paused and turned, and waited for her to catch up. When she had, he glowered, and the storm that had been brewing reached its momentum and rolled in.

"Are you insane or just naive?" he asked, his temper finally leaking into his voice. "Because following a man home—a man you don't know, I might add—isn't very smart. Or safe. Or logical. Or anything you should be doing."

"Logical, no. I'll give you that one," she said calmly, even though he had a point, even though her heart was now pumping so hard, she could hear the beat of it inside her head. "But

I'm neither insane nor naive, and I'm able to decide what I should and should not do all on my own. In case you were wondering."

"You don't know me," he repeated, pacing in sort of a half circle in front of her, his boots stirring up mini dust clouds with each step. "Where is your sense of self-preservation? Of caution? Look around you, Haley. Look!"

She didn't, just kept her focus on him. She'd seen enough driving in, and she knew exactly what he was getting at. Other than the long, skinny, dirt driveway, they were pretty much surrounded by trees. The closest neighbor was several miles down the road, and from where they stood, Gavin's house—as it sat back a ways, behind more trees—wasn't all the way visible.

In all likelihood, she could scream at the top of her lungs and not a soul would hear. But she wasn't afraid, of the remoteness or of Gavin. Angry or not, she was certain he wouldn't hurt her. As certain as she was of her height, her name, the color of the sky and the scent of freshly baked bread. The knowledge sat inside her with the same solidity, and she didn't question it.

"My sense of self-preservation is alive and well, thank you very much," she said with all the dignity she could muster. "And I happen to have very good instincts about people. I wouldn't have come here if I'd had any worries in that regard. I'm not an idiot."

"Didn't say you were an idiot," he conceded. "But there's more than one kind of smart, and I'm guessing that no one knows where you are, that you followed a strange man home to a fairly secluded area. I'm guessing that you didn't give a thought to letting even one person in on where you were headed, what you were doing. Would those be accurate assumptions?"

"Um, yes. But—"

"That's a problem," he inserted, halting his pacing. "I'm stronger than you, bigger than you, and dammit, Haley, a different man, a dangerous man, could and would take advantage of such a situation." He cursed again, rather colorfully. "So I find it hard to believe that you have even an ounce of self-preservation in your entire body, otherwise you would not be here now."

This exchange, all of it, felt more familiar than it should. Somehow, that flared her own temper into being. Narrowing her eyes, she said, "Yep, you are bigger and stronger, but I know how to protect myself. And yep, you live in a secluded area. Lots of folks around here live in seclusion. There's nothing new about that, but Gavin, you are not a different man. You are you, and—" she lifted her chin, met his gaze with hers "—you are not a dangerous man."

"You do not know that!"

"I do know that!" And she did, whether she could put the whys for that into words or not. Maybe she was an idiot, after all. Why hadn't she just phoned him? Everything was spiraling out of control, and she could only blame herself and her stupid heart-on-sleeve tendencies.

"You can't know that," he fired back.

"But I do! Sure, following you home was overkill, so I totally get your side on this." She stopped and gave herself a mental shake. "I'm sorry for that, really. It was an impulse, I guess. I just wanted to talk to you, and I saw you in your truck, and…here I am."

"I see." He stared at her, she stared right back, and somewhere in the few seconds that passed, some of the tension dissipated and a faint glimmer of humor teased into his expression, lightening the storm in his gaze. And her heart melted all over again. "Do you typically have a difficult time controlling your impulses?" he asked. "Or is this something new?"

"You're the first man I've ever followed home," she admitted. "So that's new. But I've been known to drive to the store at two in the morning for chocolate chip cookie dough ice cream when the impulse strikes, and I've perhaps made a few rash decisions here and there."

Such as when she got the bug to drive to Vegas after a late-night study session in college. But she hadn't eloped, even when the opportunity presented itself, even though she'd considered it. *That* was an impulse she'd controlled just fine.

"Look, Haley, you don't know me—"

"You've made that clear. Abundantly." She almost said she wanted to get to know him. Almost asked him to please, please allow her the gift of getting to know him, but she didn't.

"Even so, the fact remains that if I were a different type of a man, this could have ended badly," he said in a slow, purposeful beat. "A lot of people in this world aren't nice. And I hate the thought of anything bad—" Here, he broke off, as if the words he'd planned on saying got stuck in his throat. "You need to be more careful."

"Message received." Another staring competition ensued, and the moment also seemed familiar, almost intimate. When she couldn't keep the words inside any longer, she said, "I like you, Gavin. I can't explain why, so don't ask. But I like you, okay? Sue me."

His head reeled back, but he didn't drop his focus. "You're maddening. Absolutely maddening," he said under his breath. "And while I can't say for sure, it seems to me you might want to work on controlling your impulsive nature, before you find yourself in trouble."

"There's nothing wrong with a little trouble. The right type of trouble, anyway."

Out of nowhere, the idle thought came to her that if Gavin

had been the one proposing in Vegas, she might not have been able to resist. Something else to think about. Later.

"No such thing as the right sort of trouble," he said.

"I beg to differ." Determined to eke more light from the darkness, she winked and donned a bright smile. "But I admit you've made several valid points, and I'll take your advice under consideration the next time I have the impulse to trail someone."

"Uh-huh. Why don't I believe you?"

"Now you sound like my brothers." And God, did he ever. Not necessarily a bad thing. Her brothers were rocks, solid and dependable. Of course, she didn't view Gavin in a brotherly way, but she felt no need to share that information with him.

"Your brothers sound wise," Gavin said after a slight pause. "And like they love you."

"They do, and I love them. But let's keep that wise part between us, shall we?"

Something close to a grin appeared, and oh, how she yearned to see him with a real smile. With nothing but happiness in his eyes, instead of shadows. That also would be a gift.

"You're something else, Haley Foster," he said after a long, assessing moment. "What the something is, I haven't quite decided, but…something."

"You mentioned that. Earlier." Then, she'd thought he meant it as a compliment. Now, she wasn't so sure. "Ten minutes, Gavin. Can you give me that? Please?"

He sighed. "You aren't going to leave otherwise, are you?"

"No." She lifted her chin another stubborn inch. "Not until you hear me out. Ten minutes," she wheedled. "Tops."

"Does anyone ever say no to you?"

"Yes. Fairly often, in fact." Usually, though, she found ways to sidestep those noes until they became yeses. Or simply pretended she hadn't heard the no to begin with. "Feel free to say no. Really. Doesn't mean I'll hear it, though."

"I figured as much," he mumbled in resignation. "Go on, then. Say whatever it is you came here to say before I change my mind."

Mentally, she pumped her fist in the air and did the victory dance. In reality, she reminded herself to take it slow. Careful. She started with, "I surprised you when I offered to help at the Beanery. Sometimes, I get ahead of myself, and I didn't handle that all that well."

"Agreed" was all he said. But the corners of his mouth curved upward the slightest amount, and that... Well, that was a start, and she'd take it. "Go on."

"I would like to explain myself more fully, and then, once I have, I'm hoping you'll reconsider. I am serious about this, and I already have a few ideas, and I think—"

"Nope," he said instantly, quietly. "Don't think I'll be reconsidering, though I appreciate your...perseverance."

"Really, Gavin? You won't hear me out?"

"No reason to." Another barely there shake of his head. "There isn't anything you could say on this topic that would make a difference."

"You don't know that." When he started to object, she rushed forward, saying, "You might think so, but you don't. And while I can't guarantee my family will agree to a...collaboration, I guess that's the word, I think it's a possibility worth looking into."

"We'll have to agree to disagree." Calm, collected. But the hint of a grin was gone.

"Okay, look," she said hurriedly, before he ordered her to leave again. "Even if they don't want to move forward, I can still help. With the flyers and other advertising, your website, and I can certainly help get the word out. I'm pretty good at that stuff."

"Which again brings up the question—why?" Before she could reply, he held up a hand. "That question doesn't require an answer, and I shouldn't have asked it. I've heard enough. Some things are just the way they are. Some people do better on their own. Simple as that."

"Nothing is that simple."

"This is. Seriously, Haley, I think it's...generous to be so giving, but relying on others isn't my thing. Period. Never has been, never will be, and I don't see that changing."

"Ever?"

"Ever," he confirmed, without doubt or hesitation.

Well, hell. His conviction was clear and absolute. She couldn't deny it, even though she wished she could. There was nothing else to do or say, nothing at all that would change his mind, to even convince him to listen to her. And strangely, the realization hurt.

Strangely, she had the sense of almost achieving something of great worth, and the loss of that indefinable something weighed heavily inside, in the air, in every breath she took.

Yeah, it hurt. More than she understood.

"I feel sorry for you," she said softly. "Because I'm a good person, and I believe you're a good person, and yeah, I definitely have impulse-control issues. But, Gavin, here I am, offering to help. Offering you...friendship, and you're too proud or stubborn or something else, something I can't identify, to even try. And I think that's sad."

He didn't respond. Didn't look as if he were even breathing, as if he even cared that she'd put herself out there. Well, why would he? Why *should* he? As he'd said over and over and over, she didn't know him. And, well, he didn't know her. In his head, she was just some crazy chick who'd had the audacity to follow him home. Really, she couldn't blame him.

It was her turn to walk away, and so she did. The sensation of that incredible loss stayed with her as she trekked back to her car. In this scenario, she knew she'd misfired. There were so many other ways she could have gone about this. Better ways. More logical ways.

Hindsight, she decided, was the devil.

She tried to tell herself that she was being silly and over-emotional. Maybe even believed both to a certain degree. But when she tried to convince herself that, perhaps, Gavin's refusal was for the best, and she'd see the wisdom of his rejection down the road someday, she couldn't buy into the mind-set. All of this just felt wrong.

Almost heartbreakingly so.

At her car, she stopped for a second to regain her balance. Birds were singing, tree branches swayed and the cool bite of the wind touched her cheeks. All of which served to settle her mind and ease her whipped-up emotions. She hadn't done anything wrong. She'd tried. Which, really, was about all anyone could do. There wasn't any reason to kick herself over it.

Not for very long, at any rate.

She'd stop at the store for a pint of ice cream, go home, find another movie to watch or a book to read. Settle in and relax. By nightfall, she'd have put her encounter with Gavin into the proper, noncrazy perspective and she would return to normal. Hopefully, the nonitchy, nonrestless state of normal. If not, she'd go back to waiting for summer and twelve-hour workdays.

A sensible plan, for sure. She reached for the car door, her intent to follow through, when a hand lightly gripped her shoulder. Her muscles froze and her heart picked up speed. Heat flared and wove its way through her limbs, raising goose bumps on her skin and warming her from the inside out, inch by delicious inch. He'd followed her? Wow…just wow.

"Why do you want to be my friend?" Gavin asked slowly, hesitantly, from behind her. "What—what propelled you to make such a decision when you have no idea who I am?"

She didn't turn, didn't move, didn't even take in air. "I don't know, not fully," she said, going with honesty. "There's something about you that calls to me, and I want to know what that something is. I want to get to know you, and I... Well, I think...that is, I believe, that you're a person very much worth getting to know. If you'll let me."

His hand tightened on her shoulder. Not a lot, but enough to know that her words had impacted him on some level. Silence enveloped her, them, for what could have been one second or a million years. Tracking the passage of time became inconsequential.

Then the deep rumble of his voice hit her ears again. "If the offer still stands, I'd like to take you up on it. The friendship part, if not the other."

Tears, unbidden and totally unexpected, filled Haley's eyes. This admittance was also important, also held weight and conviction. And she felt every ounce of that importance, that weight and conviction to the tips of her toes. In her heart, as well.

Maybe even in her soul.

"That is an offer that doesn't have an expiration date," she said, purposely keeping her tone light and breezy. "So yes, Gavin, the offer very much still stands."

"Okay, then," he said. And darn if she didn't hear surprise and disbelief in those two little words. That was fine. He'd discover soon enough that she didn't tend to say anything she didn't mean. "Are you hungry?" he asked, still hesitant, still disbelieving. "I could make us some lunch, if you are. If you'd like to stay for a while."

"Starving, actually." One breath in, and then another, and she dropped her keys in her purse. Twisted her body toward the mountain man, looked into his gray-blue eyes, and pieces somewhere deep inside that she hadn't known were broken became connected, and the world felt…whole. She smiled. "I would love to stay. What's on the menu?"

"Ah…I guess I don't know. Let's go see what I have."

He reached for her hand, stopped midmotion. Looked at her with uncertainty and something else—yearning, she decided—and a few more broken pieces reconnected. The odd sensation of a great loss disappeared. Yes, this man was important. Vitally so.

For now, she brought her hand to his and squeezed. He nodded, tightened his grip on hers, and together they walked hand in hand toward his house, neither speaking.

Logic be damned. Because she knew, in a way she had never known one other thing in her life thus far, that this connection was what she'd been waiting for. All of her loneliness, itchiness, restlessness came down to this, to one man, to Gavin Daugherty.

He was the reason. *He* was the cure.

He was who she'd been waiting for. She *knew* it. When the Fosters fell, they fell hard. And they fought just as hard for what and who they believed in, cared for, loved. Too soon by a large margin to declare love for Gavin, but the promise of that emotion was there.

Sure. Strong. Real.

And in this moment, with her hand clasped in his, with the sun shining on their shoulders, the promise, the potential of love, was more than enough. It was a beginning, maybe *their* beginning. So she would hope she was right, she would hope that Gavin had also been waiting for her, even if he hadn't recognized her just yet. She would believe and hope he would.

It was, after all, the Foster way.

Chapter Four

A sane man didn't willingly invite a hurricane into his home, but somehow, Gavin thought he had done just that by asking Haley to stay for lunch. What had he been thinking? Well, he hadn't thought. The invitation had shot from his mouth before his brain had grasped on to the numerous—not to mention, sticky—ramifications.

And she'd said yes. So now the expectation was that he'd feed her. Talk to her. And that right there was enough to make him sweat.

He blinked and tried to focus on the contents of the cupboard he'd opened instead of the kick of acid in his stomach. Lunch wasn't a big deal. Or it shouldn't be. But the kitchen was torn apart, stuck in the middle of a renovation Gavin hadn't come close to finishing. Everything functioned, but he'd ripped out the tile, had painstakingly removed three layers of peeling wallpaper and, yesterday, had started the process of sanding the walls.

In other words, the room was a disaster. A dusty, not-fit-for-entertaining-anyone, let-alone-a-woman, let-alone-a-woman-like-Haley, disaster.

The real problem, though, was that he hadn't shopped yet this week, so his pantry was just about bare. Three cans of tomato soup, one mostly empty jar of peanut butter, half a loaf of bread—just this side of stale—and two cans of pork and beans stared back at him.

Not just bare offerings, but dismal.

"This wasn't a good idea," he muttered to himself. Closing the cupboard door with a hard snap, he shook off the descending cloud of humiliation—he had nothing to be ashamed of—and said, "As you can see, the kitchen isn't exactly fit, and I forgot I haven't shopped this week. Unless you have a hankering for pork and beans, I think we should plan this for another day."

Or never. Because really, regardless of her words about friendship or the intense way those words had hit him, they had nothing in common. Would never have anything in common. No reason to start something that wouldn't have any place to go. Right. That made sense. A solid mix of relief and regret stirred in his gut, equal in strength. He didn't allow himself time to dwell on either. In less than five minutes, Haley would leave. He'd sort out the rest on his own.

"Don't be silly," she said. "Even I can see that you're revamping the kitchen, and I don't mind a little mess. Remember, I grew up with three brothers." She stepped up behind him, so damn close he got a strong whiff of her shampoo. Apple, he guessed.

"That's kind of you," he said, recognizing—and hating—the note of desperation in his voice. "Doesn't alter the fact I don't have any real food in the house."

"I'm not a picky eater." Reaching around him as if she hadn't heard him, as if she'd stood in this kitchen every blessed day of her life, she opened the cupboard door he'd just shut. His desperation doubled. "Look, there's plenty to choose from. There's nothing to worry about."

"I wouldn't call *plenty* an accurate description. And who said I was worried?"

"Sufficient, then," she said. "And you looked worried, with the way your face was all scrunched up and how you kept pulling at your beard."

"The beard itches," he retorted. True enough, but her comment made him self-conscious. "My face was not scrunched up, and I'm not worried. At all."

"Good. Because you shouldn't be. You have tomato soup, and if we add a couple of grilled cheese sandwiches, we'll have an excellent lunch. One of my favorites, actually."

He blinked again. Yup, a freaking hurricane. Maybe not a category nine, but he'd wager a solid six. Possibly as high as a seven.

"Mine, as well." What, exactly, would it take to dissuade this woman? Trying again, in a resolute, no-arguments-accepted tone, he said, "Difficult, though, to make grilled cheese sandwiches without cheese. Or butter. So again, I think it would be best to put this off until—"

"I'm here. You're here. I'm starving, so I'm sure we can come up with something," she said stubbornly, her gaze fixated on the cupboard, as if a team of elves had miraculously stocked his shelves in the past thirty seconds. "Besides which, you invited me. Remember?"

"That I did, though at the moment I can't quite recall why."

"Doesn't matter," she said with a fair amount of amusement. "Would be unfair to back out now. Rude, too. You wouldn't want that, now would you? Not when I'm starving and all."

He scratched at his beard, realized what he was doing and stopped. Stared at the back of her head. Unfair and rude, huh?

She had him good and stuck. It seemed that nothing short of an actual hurricane would get her out of his kitchen. He should be annoyed, ready to physically carry her from his home. Instead, he felt something reminiscent of pleasure at her insistence.

Another sensation he refused to dwell on.

Shaking his head, he metaphorically held up his hands in surrender. "I guess not, seeing as you're starving. And here, apparently refusing to leave."

With these words, her entire body seemed to soften and she expelled a short breath. Somehow, these small details didn't escape Gavin's attention. A fact that didn't set him at ease or help loosen the hard knot of apprehension in his gut. She rattled him, plain and simple.

Every last thing about her.

"Well, I think we'll stick with the tomato soup and exchange the grilled cheese sandwiches for peanut butter toast," she said as she grabbed the necessary items and deposited them on the counter. "Sounds perfect, don't you think?"

Peanut butter and tomato in the same meal? Closer to revolting, but he wasn't about to argue. All that would do was prolong this visit. "Sure," he drawled. "Absolutely perfect."

"And here you were, about to send me away for no reason at all."

"Can't imagine what I was thinking."

"Me, either." Nodding toward the refrigerator, she said, "May I?"

Shocked she'd even bothered to ask, he shrugged. "Seems you're in charge here, so why not? Though you won't find much. I don't keep a lot of supplies on hand."

"Typical bachelor." Without pause, she opened the fridge, took stock of its contents—also meager—and pulled out the milk and two containers of yogurt. "For dessert," she said.

"What? No appetizers?"

"Wow, was that a joke, Mr. Serious?"

"More like ill-timed sarcasm," he said. Remorse crept in, overriding every other conflicting emotion he had going. She was here because he'd invited her to be here. Wasn't her fault he didn't know how to deal with people. "Sorry. I shouldn't have said that."

"Why? I appreciate a good one-liner."

"Right. Well, um, I guess—"

"Tell you what," she broke in, obviously noticing his discomfort. "I'll heat up the soup if you get me a saucepan. I can't cook much, but I can handle canned soup without too much difficulty."

"Nope." He didn't know a lot about entertaining, but he knew a guest shouldn't do the cooking. "You're a guest. Sit down. I'll cook."

"I don't sit well for very long," she countered. "You'll have to give me a job, or—" she paused and a glimmer of light appeared in the depths of her eyes "—actually, that's a fine idea. I can sit back and relax, ask you questions while you cook. I have a ton of them."

And then, she actually winked at him. Winked!

"No!" he damn near yelled. Whatever questions Miss Haley Foster might find appropriate to ask, he wasn't prepared to hear—or answer. He didn't know her well, but he'd seen enough of her personality to have zero doubts on this front. She'd go for the personal, and he didn't do personal. With anyone. "I, uh, a job, huh?"

"Yes, please," she said sweetly, with a bat of her eyelashes.

"I guess you could set the table. Toast the bread, too, if you'd like." She grinned, wide and...saucy. Since when he had started using terms like *saucy* to describe a woman's smile? Glancing away, he said, "Will that be enough to keep you from sitting still for too long?"

"Works for me," she agreed in the same sweet way. "I'll

just save my questions until we're eating. It'll be more fun talking then, anyway. And you'll be able to pay more attention."

He rubbed his hands over his face, resisted the urge to yank at his beard. If he wasn't absolutely positive he stood on solid ground, he'd have sworn the floor shook and swayed. "You do that," he said, gruffer than he'd intended. "Don't set your hopes too high, though. I'm not what is known as a chatty guy."

"Again, this proves how well we'll get along. I am very chatty."

"There's a shocker," he said.

"And another one-liner!" Her lips quirked again, and he readied himself for whatever she was going to throw at him next. "I bet that you're far more sociable than you think you are."

"You'd lose that bet."

"Hmm. I'm a decent judge of character."

"Decent isn't perfect, and I'd bet I know myself better than you."

"Maybe." A flyaway strand of hair fell into her eyes. She pursed her lips, puffed, and the strand of hair blew to the side. "Maybe not."

If she were his to touch, he'd walk over, pull that contraption from her hair, and— *Stop,* he ordered his brain, *right now.* Damn good advice, that, so he tossed the words, the image, as far away as possible and searched for balance. Peace. And found none.

She stared at him, her eyes filled with curiosity, and he was positive that she did have the ability to see right into his head, to read every last thought he had. Coughing to break the moment, the intensity of her gaze, he pointed toward the cupboard on the other side of the stove. "Dishes are there. You'll find silverware in the drawer below. I don't have fancy stuff."

Now, why'd he have to go and say something like that?

"I'm not a fancy girl." With a smart-alecky salute and a sashay of her hips, she walked to where he'd pointed. "Napkins?"

"Nope. I use paper towels."

She nodded, but didn't say anything else. Saving it up, he was sure. Should he talk? Probably. About what? He fought to find some topic of conversation that would make it appear as if he were comfortable and not ready to jump clean out of his skin. Nothing worthwhile came to mind, so he quit thinking and focused on his one and only task: heating the darn soup. The sooner they ate, the sooner she'd leave, the sooner he'd be able to breathe again.

They worked around each other, neither speaking. He heard her gather the dishes and silverware, and just as at the Beanery, he felt her presence even when he couldn't see her. She had an energy that was, at once, vivid and warm. Saturating and, yes, life-affirming. It bounced around the room, around him, in a way that somehow made him feel more whole. Real.

Dammit all. She really did remind him of the sun.

The thought didn't sit with him any better than it had before, so he inhaled a deep breath into his lungs and stirred the soup. Kept right on stirring, because he wasn't sure what else to do with himself. He should've let her take care of the soup, as she'd wanted. Then, at least, he'd have been mobile and not stuck inside his own head making ridiculous comparisons. Next time, he'd let her— No. There wouldn't be a next time.

Couldn't be a next time when he wasn't sure he would survive *this* time.

Suddenly, there she was, standing beside him and putting the bread into the toaster. Too close for comfort. A weird sense of familiarity appeared. Almost like déjà vu. If he let himself, he might be able to believe that this—preparing a meal, sharing space with each other—had happened before. Many, many times before. And would happen again.

That was asinine, and about as illogical as everything else that had occurred since the moment she'd fallen into line behind him at the coffee shop. Illogical and meaningless.

He stirred harder, stared into the pan as if it were a crystal ball and an answer would magically appear. Or a way out. Anything, really, that would get him through however long it would take for Haley to eat, ask her questions and vamoose.

In far too few minutes, the soup finished heating. Gavin turned off the burner, brought the pan to the table and awkwardly filled their bowls. "Soup's done," he said over his shoulder.

She was right there, with two glasses of milk in her hands. They jostled around each other, and again, he caught the scent of her shampoo. Fruity, yes, but not apple. Whatever the fragrance was, he liked it. Thought maybe he could get used to that scent.

Maybe even to the woman herself.

And that had come from precisely nowhere. Shaking off that tidbit of idiocy, he put down the pan, grabbed the toast and returned to the table, where she was already seated. Anxiety crawled along his skin, whispered into his tense muscles. Why the hell had he asked her for lunch? He wasn't that good at social interaction with anyone, ever. Never had been.

"Are you going to sit, or stare at the table?" Haley asked.

"Just making sure we have everything," he said stiffly. And since he couldn't see any way out of the predicament, he took the chair across from her, and said the first words that came to mind. "Thank you for helping."

"Welcome. Thank you for inviting me." She spread a glob of peanut butter on a slice of toast, offered him the jar. "Even if you did try to rescind the invitation."

"You managed to wiggle right out of that one," he said,

accepting the jar and setting it aside. No way, no how was he going to pair peanut butter toast with tomato soup. "Most folks would've just agreed and set up another date. You—"

"I'm not most people." She folded her toast in half, so it made a sandwich, dunked it in her soup and took a large bite. Peanut butter smeared the top of her lip, which she licked clean before taking another bite. His pulse shifted into a higher gear and his mouth went dry.

He dropped his gaze. Fast. This, he decided for the second time that day, could never happen again. Not if he wanted to protect his sanity, which he very much did. A woman like Haley would drive him ten ways of crazy in no time flat. Hell, he was already halfway there.

"No, you are definitely not most people," he managed to say.

"Neither are you."

He couldn't argue with that one. "Has anyone—I don't know, your brothers, maybe—ever brought up the issue of your stubbornness? Along with your impulsive nature and lack of a self-preservation instinct, that is?"

"Now there's a question," she said with a chuckle. "Truth is, all of us Fosters have a stubborn streak a mile wide. I'm not alone in that regard."

"Only a mile, huh?" She laughed again, soft and bubbly, and the sound of that laugh forced his eyes upward. Eyelashes fluttered and in an instant, he was lost there, in the humor and joy he saw in her gaze. Crazy. "I would guess yours is at least twenty times that."

"Depends on who you ask," she said. "Some might say more, some might say less."

"What if I'm asking you?"

She wrinkled her nose. "Why aren't you eating?"

"Oh." Because he'd gotten so caught up in their conversation, in her, that he'd forgotten he was supposed to be eating. He swallowed a few bites of soup, one of dry toast and, after washing all of that down with a gulp of his milk, said, "There, now answer my question."

"I believe you've already deduced my stubbornness quotient. If something—or someone—is important to me," she said quietly, with conviction, "I will keep beating my head against a brick wall, even if doing so seems futile. I don't tend to give up."

Her message *seemed* loud and clear, but Gavin wasn't sure if he could buy into his interpretation. Deciding to take the light approach, he forced his mouth into some semblance of a smile, tried out a laugh. Sounded rusty, ill-used, to his own ears. "Seems as if you'd walk around with a headache most of the time, going about life in such a fashion."

"Sometimes," she agreed. "But I'd rather have the headache than the knowledge I gave up." Reaching over, she squeezed his hand. Quicklike. "I guess you should know I don't give up all that often. Takes an awful lot to force me to walk away."

He busied himself with his soup, unsure of how to respond. Or even if he should. The room became quiet as they ate, and he realized his earlier discomfort had lessened by a few degrees. When, exactly, had his stress level dropped? When had he become more at ease with Haley than he had with any other person in a long, long while?

The answer eluded him, but this—as odd and disconcerting as the facts were—gave him pause, something to consider. Her words, as well. Maybe getting to know Haley would prove to be the beginning of finding his place, a true home, here in Steamboat Springs. He wanted that. Very much so. More than that, he yearned for a connection. Something real with another person.

Friendship. The concept seemed too big to take in, made his heart gallop in his chest all over again. There was warmth there, too, slipping and sliding through his bloodstream in a way he'd never before experienced. Startling but not unwelcome. Frightening, but he could deal with that. Or he thought he could, if given enough time and space.

"Haley," he said, before he could talk himself out of it, "I'm glad you stayed."

"I'm glad I stayed, too. So," she said, rubbing her hands together, "are you ready for my first question? I have three or four all lined up and ready to go."

The prospect still seemed daunting. Terrifying. But maybe not quite so much. "Only three or four? From what you said, I expected…oh, a hundred. Maybe two hundred."

"Way more than that," she said, her expression serious and intent. "But you and I? We're just getting started, Gavin. I see no reason to rush anything. We have plenty of time ahead of us."

Just getting started. Plenty of time. Us.

A bolt of his earlier anxiety returned but he didn't pay heed to it, didn't give the negativity room to grow. He wanted this. Wanted to have the opportunity to get to know Haley, wanted to find it in himself to allow her to get to know him. Even if the whole idea scared him witless. Even if she—and her motivation—confused the hell out of him. He wanted this.

Maybe, he even needed this.

"So, are you ready?" she asked again.

"I believe I am," he said, praying hard that he was, indeed, ready. "Fire away."

Scowling, Haley pushed her hair off her forehead and let loose a string of colorful curse words. All of which her brothers had taught her at one point or another. Last month's numbers for the sports store refused to balance, and darn if she could figure out why.

The mistake, she knew, was likely hers. An inputting error

or something equally simple. She just couldn't find it, and didn't think she had much left in her for the night. Her head ached, she couldn't see straight and her shoulders were sore from leaning over the computer at an awkward angle for so freaking long. Yeah, she was done.

Releasing a sigh, she closed her eyes and pushed out a breath. Tomorrow, she'd phone her cousin Seth's wife, Rebecca—who thankfully was a CPA—and beg for help. Maybe even consider Rebecca's offer to take over more of the accounting. What a relief that would be. Of course, Haley's workload would drop significantly during their slow seasons, and therefore her paycheck would also drop accordingly. She'd insist on that, even if her family argued.

Not a huge deal. She lived in the apartment above the restaurant rent-free, so living on less money wouldn't cause any problems. Mostly, she just hated not being busy.

Perhaps there was more she could do at the restaurant, or maybe Cole could use extra help at the sporting goods store until the summer season kicked into full gear. She'd bring up the possibility at the next family meeting, get everyone else's take and go from there.

Opening her eyes, she saved and closed the software program. Sighed again, frustrated she hadn't been able to locate the error. She blamed Gavin. Well, that was unfair. It wasn't his fault she couldn't get him out of her head, couldn't stop thinking of him.

Lord, had that man made an impact.

Somehow, she had to find a way to bring him on board with her collaboration idea. Then, she'd have a slew of projects to focus on. Even better, she'd have plenty of reasons to spend time with the mountain man. Getting a new business up and running, even a small business, would require hours and hours of work. Side by side, talking, figuring out all of the details.

Learning what made him tick.

She'd be useful, too, if he'd let her. Valuable. Her degree was in business marketing, but she had a knack for design and enjoyed the creative process, coming up with ideas. For starters, he needed a logo. Well-designed brochures, flyers, an entire online presence. And he also needed to get to know more of the locals. Word-of-mouth could go a long, long way.

Joining forces with the Fosters would help. Her family was already well-known, had already formed the necessary connections. She'd even figured out how a partnership with Gavin could benefit her family's businesses. They always had clients they had to turn away during the busy seasons. If Gavin and her family agreed, they could refer these folks to each other.

New business would mean repeat business in following seasons, at least to a certain extent, and that meant a better bottom line. Even if the benefits fell more on Gavin's side.

Unfortunately, she couldn't do one thing with any of her ideas unless Gavin and her family agreed. There was a solution, somewhere. Haley just hadn't found it yet, but she would. She could be awfully stubborn when something mattered.

The now-familiar warmth balled low in her stomach, flared through her limbs. Gavin mattered. A lot. The feeling that he was important—possibly even essential—to her life hadn't lessened. If anything, her belief in this regard had grown stronger. More certain.

For now, though, she was keeping all of this to herself. Her family, as much as she loved them and vice versa, were a nosy, intrusive crew, dipping into one another's lives without hesitation. Heck, she was the same way with them, so she couldn't really complain.

But this connection with Gavin—whatever that turned out to be—demanded space to grow without interference. Specifically, her brothers' interference. She could only imagine how Gavin would react if Reid, Dylan, Cole—or, good grief, all three of them—showed up on his doorstep playing their overprotective big-brother roles. If this were to happen, she'd be lucky to ever hear from him again. He'd likely take off at a dead run if he ever saw her coming.

And once gone, she had a feeling he'd never look back.

Better for now to keep this sense of finding something—*someone*—special, a secret. Wouldn't be easy, though. Not with her family. Not in Steamboat Springs, either, where everyone knew her. Well, then. She'd have to make the best use of whatever time she had before the secret was out in the open. And really, why not start now?

Haley glanced at her cell, willing it to ring. Didn't work, naturally. She'd hoped, after their lunch, that Gavin would contact her. Four days later, and she hadn't heard from him. Should she practice patience as well as secrecy and give him a little longer, see if he used the phone number she'd left with him? Or should she contact him?

The answer was clear and immediate. Without giving the idea any additional consideration, she pulled out the flyer from her desk, where she'd stashed it, and logged in to her email program. What could be more cautious and nonintrusive than a freaking email?

Seemed safe, low-key. Far better than following him home, which surprisingly hadn't ended in disaster. If he responded to her email, she'd go from there.

If he didn't, she'd proceed in a different direction. A cautious, secretive-to-her-family, nonimpulsive direction that hopefully wouldn't send Gavin running for the hills.

She chewed on her bottom lip, twisted her hair around her finger and considered the probability of her being able to remain cautious, secretive and patient all at the same time.

Right. She was so screwed.

Chapter Five

Another question, Gavin thought, staring at the email message that had popped into his in-box less than fifteen minutes ago. Lord, the woman had a million and one questions, and he figured once he'd answered all of those, she'd find another million to toss his way.

Not that he minded all that much. He just didn't understand how someone could have such a high curiosity about another person. He never had. Well, he corrected, that used to be true. As it turned out, he found himself mighty curious about one Haley Foster. Not that he'd bounced the question ball back in her direction. Couldn't quite seem to do it, even when he'd typed his question out, all nice and neat. Something—nerves, doubt—always made him delete that bit before sending the message on. Eventually, maybe. For now, he was just fine with the status quo.

Okay, perhaps fine was an overexaggeration of sorts.

Thirteen days had passed since they'd shared a meal, and

for most of the hours in the first four of those days, he'd had this squirrely, jumpy, almost-but-not-quite panicky sensation that he'd dreamed up the whole encounter. Or that she'd decided he wasn't worth the effort to get to know, despite what she'd said, and was sorry she'd given in to the impulse to follow him home.

To combat those negative thoughts, because he didn't fully believe them even if they did stick in his head like glue, he'd readied himself to pick up the phone. To call her.

Only problem was, he had no idea what to say.

After some thinking on that, when he had a few ideas toward having an actual conversation—a conversation that he would instigate, no less—and was all set to give those ideas a shot, she'd surprised him with an email. In the time since then, they'd developed a routine. She would email, ask him a question or two, and he would respond.

It seemed she'd been honest. It seemed she hadn't changed her mind. She really did want to get to know him. The reality of it all took some getting used to. He was almost there. Almost believing in something that both scared him and made him, if not happy, optimistic.

How was that even possible? How could any one thing—particularly, a woman—cause two emotions that were about as opposite as two things can get? He didn't know. Didn't much care to put a magnifying glass on the reasons, either. One day a time...hell, one email at a time, was about all a man could handle when the woman in question was Haley Foster.

Even so, he couldn't stop the smile that appeared as he reread Haley's latest message, at the now-familiar punch of surprise that hit him anew. Where did she come up with this stuff? Last Christmas was months ago, the next was a greater number of months away, so why this question now? And did it really matter to her what his favorite Christmas memory was?

Another negative thought. He pushed that one out before

it could take hold, before the slenderest strand of negativity could shake his equilibrium or do away with his contentment. She'd gone to the trouble of asking, hadn't she? Yep, she had. Apparently, whether he understood it or not, his favorite Christmas memory mattered to her. Well, then.

Wasn't hard to find the answer. Most of his Christmases hadn't held even a zip of magic or wonder. There were a few, though, that had. One in particular. One that he'd never forget.

Gavin started to type. Stopped. Thought about which words to use, which order to put those words in, how to express what was in his head and, maybe even more important, his heart, without sounding cheesy. Or dumb. Or... Dammit. Why did he do this to himself?

"Quit thinking so much and just answer the friggin' question," he muttered. So, typing with one finger, he wrote his message in simple terms:

My favorite Christmas memory, huh? I suppose that would have to be the year we had a new puppy in the house. She used her teeth to open most every present under the tree before any of us got up. Bits of paper were all over the place. That pup made one helluva mess. It was funny. I guess that's why it's my favorite. Laughing on Christmas morning seems like a good thing. Was a good thing.

Gavin stared at what he'd written, second-guessed himself a thousand times and, when he couldn't think of a better way to say what he'd already said, finally hit Send. Good enough, he supposed, but he hadn't quite admitted the truth, hadn't shared the real reason why this particular memory meant so much to him. Why he'd never let it go.

Rubbing his beard, which he hadn't yet trimmed, he allowed himself a minute to dip into the memory. He'd been twelve that year, had only lived with the Demkos since the previous August, so this was the first of three Christmases he was lucky enough to spend with them.

He'd moved in right before school had started, which hadn't pleased him any. Different schools so often might have become normal, but that didn't mean he'd ever grown used to being the new kid. So he had the tough, surly attitude, the feigned distaste for anything and everything Russ and Elaine tried to do for him, show him, buy him.

They'd treated him well. Real well, and what had he done in return? Yelled, stormed off, skipped school, stole money from Russ's wallet for no reason other than he could and pretty much anything else he could think of to get a rise out of them. And yeah, he'd managed to do that a time or two, but they never threatened to send him away. They just kept trying to get through the barriers he'd built around himself, and he kept promising they never would.

And then Christmas morning arrived. He'd had the wish the night before that his mother would get her act together and show up just in time to spend the holiday with her son. She hadn't, but by then, he'd stopped thinking about her so much. Because that morning, seeing that pup—Roxie, her name had been Roxie—with wrapping paper hanging out of her mouth, torn shreds of it all over the floor, dangling lights and fallen ornaments, and boxes with the corners chewed off, had done something to him. Something he couldn't explain, other than to say he'd laughed, along with Russ and Elaine, along with the other kid staying with them.

And that laughter, the mess around him, that silly pup, all but smashed the shield he'd erected. Now, today, he shook his head, smiling all over again, caught in the memory. That was the moment he'd relaxed enough to start letting Russ and Elaine in. That was the moment he'd first started to learn what being a part of a family—a real, honest-to-God family—entailed.

He'd never forgotten that day, that memory. Not once.

That morning had changed him as no other morning, no other Christmas ever had. But how in the world could he explain that to another person, a person who probably had a happy memory for every Christmas she'd been alive? In an email, for crying out loud?

The moment was too big for words, he guessed. Too much to explain to someone who wouldn't be able to understand the concept of not having a real family.

Gavin swore under his breath. Stared at his email. Debated the wisdom of what he was thinking of, told himself again to stop all the thinking and did it. Wrote another email to Haley, this one with enough words and details, hopefully, to get his point across, without going into too much detail. Without sharing the pain that came before and later.

And then, dammit, he couldn't move from the fold-out chair or stop staring at the laptop screen. Not until she responded, not until he was sure he hadn't exposed too much.

Five...ten...twenty minutes passed before the telltale new-message "click" went off. Twenty excruciating minutes filled with absolute certainty that he should've kept his mouth shut and not shared what he'd just shared. No way would she understand.

He almost ignored the message. Hell, she'd have no clue when he'd check his email again. But he couldn't do it; he had to know if she'd gotten the point of what he'd tried so hard to say. Why he cared so much, he didn't know. If she didn't understand, the lack wouldn't be any fault of hers. It would be a mix of her own upbringing and his inability to convey a moment he'd never before attempted to put into words.

Also, though, he didn't want her pity. Didn't want anyone's pity, really, but most especially not hers. Nervous, Gavin double-clicked on the message. Swallowed hard, and read:

Thank you, Gavin, for trusting me enough to share this. I feel honored to know this about you, your life. But, wow, I'm so glad you had Russ and Elaine. So very happy you have this memory.
—Haley
P.S. Curious: What are your favorite pizza toppings?

Gavin read the message no less than four times before a swell of…well, he didn't exactly know what to call this particular emotion…overtook him. Whatever it was, it felt good, he knew that. He'd told someone something about his past, something real, and that someone—Haley—had understood. In his mind, that was pretty darn incredible.

His eyes fell on the P.S. she'd written, and he grinned. Pizza toppings, huh? This time, he didn't have to worry about what words to use or what order to put them in. This was the simplest question yet.

Easier to say what I don't like: anchovies. Anything else is good with me. And you're welcome. About the sharing.

With that, he hit Send and returned to the kitchen to sand the walls. A task he'd ignored for too long in favor of a handful of outdoor projects, and since he had longer-than-normal shifts at the hardware store tomorrow and Sunday, he wouldn't have time again until next week.

A solid hour of hard work passed, but Gavin barely noticed. His thoughts were too focused on Haley, her possible motives, how she might be spending her evening and a dozen other details that shouldn't be taking up so much of his brain space.

She was still there, deeply embedded in his head, when the phone rang, and he had a split second where he was positive she was on the other end of the line.

If he'd been in his normal state of mind, he would've looked at the caller ID. Would've read the "Unknown Name/

Unknown Number" flag and would've known, without a doubt, that the person calling him wasn't Haley Foster. But he wasn't in his normal state of mind, and he didn't look, so when he answered, he was about as floored as a man could be.

"Gavin," the woman said, her voice cracking with emotion. Feigned, he was sure. Still, the familiarity of her voice and the emotion that voice held got to him. Annoying, that. She shouldn't get to him. Not anymore. "Don't hang up, please. I'd like the chance to talk with you, and you never seem to be around when I call. Or you don't answer."

Jerking the phone down, he read the caller ID and grimaced. Someone had apparently taught his mother how to hide her phone number. "Are you hurt?"

"No, but—"

"Did you get the check I sent last week?"

"Yes, thank you, but that isn't why—"

"You're only supposed to use this number in case of an emergency. That was what we agreed on," he reminded her. "Is there an emergency?"

"Gavin, if you could just listen to me," she said, pleaded. "That's all I want."

"Is there an emergency?" he repeated, already knowing the answer but needing to hear his mother's verification before disconnecting the call.

"No, there isn't an emergency." And dammit, there was that break in her voice, the break that typically signified that the waterworks were about to begin. "Five minutes, that's all I ask."

All she wanted, all she asked. Always, for as far back as he could remember, everything was about her. Well, not now. Not today. Not for a long time. "You ask too much."

He hung up and powered down the phone before she could say anything else or put on a show of crying. Tried to ignore the guilt he felt and failed. Considered throwing the phone against the wall, but managed to restrain the impulse.

For most of his childhood, he'd listened to and believed Vanessa Daugherty's justifications, of which she had many. A good portion of his teenage years were spent going against his common sense and *choosing* to believe in her, her excuses, her promises. It had taken him decades to learn that his mother, as much as he wished otherwise, was incapable of change.

It had taken him decades to understand that the only way to protect himself was to stop listening, stop believing, and to keep her as far out of his life as possible. But every time he heard his mother's voice, something inside railed against this decision, pushed at him to lower his shields, to listen and give her a chance. Just one more chance.

And the idea of that scared him. Angered him. How many chances did one person deserve? He supposed the number differed from person to person, from situation to situation, but in Vanessa Daugherty's case, he couldn't—wouldn't—open that door again.

Not when she had repeatedly slammed that very same door in his face, despite the many chances he'd given her. Despite how much he loved her. Despite…everything.

Gavin replaced the dust mask over his mouth, picked up the sander and got back to work. Unfortunately, his thoughts this go-around weren't as pleasant or hopeful. All he kept thinking, all that went through his head, was the simple truth: except for the years with the Demkos, life had taught him that he did better on his own.

A lesson he shouldn't allow himself to forget.

Probably, Haley thought with a grain of concern, she should have warned Gavin why she'd asked about his favorite pizza toppings, but she hadn't wanted to give him the opportunity to shoot her down. So, here she was, driving toward his house, again uninvited, with an extra-large, every-topping-under-the-sun-except-for-anchovies pizza in tow. Along with a couple of sodas, a bag of chips and two huge pieces of chocolate cake she'd snagged from the restaurant.

Another impulsive gesture, yes, but she'd had the itch to see him for... Well, ever since she last saw him. She'd ignored the compulsion just fine until tonight, when she'd learned that he'd mostly been raised in the foster care system, that his favorite Christmas memory was, in fact, his first ever happy Christmas memory—and he'd been twelve, for goodness's sake. Her heart had returned to its melted-pile-of-goo state, and she'd had to see him.

It wasn't a question, or even a want. It was *necessary* that she saw him.

Hopefully, this meal would prove less challenging than their last. Hopefully, she wouldn't have to use every tool in her arsenal in order to stay. Mostly, she believed he'd be happy to see her. Lots had changed in the time they'd been emailing. He was communicating, for one. Each and every email he responded to made her want to jump up and down and cheer. For another, each of his responses had grown slightly wordier, which to her meant he was becoming comfortable with the idea of her. Maybe even with the idea of *them*.

And friendship, regardless of what she thought might eventually exist between them, was a solid foundation on which to begin. Yes, she was pleased with their progression. Hopeful.

She'd barely pulled into Gavin's long, skinny driveway when her cell phone rang. One glance told her who the caller was—Suzette—and that was enough to bring Matt the teacher and the blind date she'd agreed to back into her memory. Oh, no. She had no desire to spend an evening with another man who wasn't Gavin Daugherty.

Well, she'd just tell Suzette the truth.

"Hey," she said into the phone as she put her car in Park.

"I'm guessing you're finally calling about this date, and the thing is, I'm not really comfortable with the idea. So—"

"No way, Haley," Suzette interrupted. "You agreed. And I've spoken with Matt and well…it took some convincing, but everything's all set for tomorrow."

"Unset it. I'm not interested." Okay, that came out a little too abrupt. "I'm sorry, but I've changed my mind. I'm sure he'll understand, since you had to 'convince' him to agree."

"You're not really going to do this to me, are you? I have to work with this guy…and see, things have finally gotten comfortable between us again."

Haley's eyes narrowed. "What do you mean things have finally gotten comfortable? What aren't you telling me?" When her friend didn't instantly respond, she said, "Spill it."

"Okay, okay." A long, drawn-out sigh. "We flirted for a few months. But we went out and nothing clicked. The chemistry wasn't there. I mean, it was for him. Just not for me."

"Ah, I see. So now, you're concerned that if I'm a no-show, your work relationship will be uncomfortable again?"

"Yes, but also…please, Haley?"

"I don't know." She would rather do almost anything else other than this, but Suzette was her friend. And tricked or not, she had agreed. "This has disaster written all over it."

"Not necessarily, and I'll owe you. One favor, anytime, for any reason, no questions asked. Please?" Suzette wheedled. "Pretty please?"

Haley closed her eyes, swore quietly. "If—and I mean *if*—I go, you have to understand that there will not be a second date. I've met someone else." She looked in the direction of Gavin's house. He was in there, and she was out here. Stuck. "Don't ask who he is, either."

Dead silence. For a good thirty seconds.

"You win," Suzette said. "I won't even beg you for more information."

And because she didn't, Haley fully grasped how important this date was to her friend. Which meant she had to go... but not without stipulations.

"Dinner only," she said. "No movie. No stopping for drinks afterward. I don't want to take a walk or play a game of pool. Dinner. That's all I'll agree to."

"Fine," Suzette said after another loud sigh. "Dinner only."

"Then we have a deal. Where and when? I'll drive myself."

Suzette begrudgingly gave her the details. Then, "So...ah, what does this mystery man of yours look like? You have to give me something here."

"Um. He has eyes and a nose and a mouth. Two legs. Hair. If I recall correctly, he also has two arms. Hands, with five fingers on each. Oh, and I'm assuming—"

"You're a snot," Suzette said with a laugh. "This will drive me crazy."

"I'll tell you who he is...eventually." Haley grinned. "But now I have to go."

They disconnected and Haley took a second to gather her bearings. Ugh. Matt the teacher was probably a very nice man. But nice or not, he wasn't Gavin. Who, Haley reminded herself, was just up the driveway a bit, and if he wasn't too surprised by her visit, tonight might become another turning point. So what in the world was she doing sitting here in her car?

With that, she balanced the pizza, slid her wrist in the straps of her purse and the handle of the to-go bag, and stepped outside. The heady concoction of anticipation, exhilaration and nervousness tingling through her body made it seem as if she were floating, rather than merely walking. Flying instead of putting one foot in front of the other on a dusty dirt driveway.

By the time she made it to his front door, the nervousness had taken center stage. She once again considered if this, showing up unexpectedly twice, was really her smartest move. But hell, she was already here, and she rarely second-guessed herself. So again, why start now?

She mentally gave herself a good shake, sucked in one breath to steady herself and—before her doubts could expand—used her elbow to press the doorbell. Breathed again. Hoped and prayed that this wasn't one of those oddball instances where her instincts would prove to be way off base. And waited.

Chapter Six

Fortunately, she didn't have to wait overly long. Gavin opened the door a scant minute or two later, with surprise and…well, an edge of defense, perhaps. He had that closed-down, shielded-to-the-world facade securely in place, easily identifiable. To her, at least.

She smiled brightly, took in the fine layer of white dust that powdered his brown-but-not-brown hair, black T-shirt and well-fitted jeans, and decided he looked very much like a man who'd been caught in a snowstorm. Sexy, though. Even with the dust. Even with the defensive attitude and shielded eyes. Tall and strong and capable.

Just the sight of him ignited the low, slow burn she was becoming so familiar with.

"You're either in the middle of baking and had an altercation with a bag of flour, or," Haley said, attempting to sound lighthearted, "you're in the process of sanding walls." The latter, she was sure, based on how the kitchen had looked when she'd been here for lunch.

"Sanding," Gavin confirmed in a short, clipped manner. "I don't know how to bake."

The bag weighed heavily against Haley's wrist, the strap biting mercilessly into her skin. The pizza box held enough warmth that the heat had started to become uncomfortable. These physical distresses, her very real nervousness and her body's response to Gavin, along with the abrupt, somewhat cool way in which he'd spoken, all seemed to state that she should've stuck with the safety of emails. Too late now.

"I brought pizza," she said hurriedly. "And drinks, dessert. For dinner."

He regarded her steadily, his surprise at finding her on his porch still apparent. Eyes narrowed, he tugged at the dust mask hanging around his neck. "Dinner? You brought dinner?"

Her stomach plummeted to her toes. He didn't sound or look pleased. Or happy. Or anything she could describe as positive. Darn it. Why had she done this?

"Yes, dinner." She blinked, forced another smile. "The meal that is typically the last of the day. Well, unless you count dessert, but that isn't really—"

"I am familiar with the concept of dinner," he said. "I'm more confused about why you're here. Did we have plans I forgot about, or…?"

"That would be a no. But, um, I don't have to stay! Just wanted to help out, since I thought you might be working on the house. Might be too busy to think of dinner." She searched for, and found, a hint of her normal courage. "Friends do this, Gavin. Promise."

"Friends bring surprise pizzas?" He reached for the box and the bag, retrieving both before she'd realized she'd passed them over. "Thanks. It was kind of you to go to the trouble."

"Wasn't any trouble, and you're welcome." Nope, there wasn't one thing to say to save this moment. Other than, "I'm sorry I didn't call first. I should have called."

"Wouldn't have done you any good. I… Phone's off right now."

"Well, I could've mentioned stopping by in that last email."

"Yup, you could've done that," he agreed. "I guess, though, there's no harm done, and I could use a break. Those walls are a pain in the as—behind."

"Breaks are good! Enjoy dinner, and—" What was wrong with her? She straightened her spine, strengthened her smile. Haley Foster did not do meek. "It's an extra-large pizza. I could stay, eat with you. Friends do that, as well. Share meals. In case you were wondering."

Again, he regarded her in that unflinching custom of his, and it was all she could do not to rescind her words. Her muscles tensed as she waited for his reply, and while she hoped he'd invite her in, she feared he wouldn't. Feared she'd taken another misstep.

"I suppose friends do share meals," he said after a long, drawn-out, excruciating pause. "And if you'd like to stay, I won't say no."

"You can, though. I'll listen this time." Boy, would she ever. "No hard feelings, either."

"If I wanted to say no, I would've said no." Was that a grin? Maybe. He stepped to the side, giving her room to enter. "This was real nice of you, and I appreciate the thoughtfulness."

"More selfish than thoughtful," she said honestly, walking past him. "I wanted to see you. Wanted to spend time with you. So I bought a pizza and here I am."

This, her statement, stopped him dead in his tracks. Pivoting, he squinted at her as if she were a bug he was trying to identify. His jaw hardened, for just a second, really, and he shook his head. Confusion glittered in his eyes, but maybe a small amount of amusement existed there, as well. Pleasure, perhaps. And if so, those were good reactions.

"Still haven't quite decided what to make of you," he admitted, his voice rough but not disbelieving. Also a positive. "Other than you haven't stopped surprising me yet."

She'd have liked more. Would have liked to hear him say that he'd wanted to see her, spend time with her, too. It was on the tip of her tongue to ask, to just put the question out there, but she decided against doing so. Later, maybe, but not now. He seemed...subdued, as if a great weight rested on his shoulders. A weight he was tired of carrying around.

In the next second, she decided she was being ridiculous. Of course he was tired. Manual labor tended to tire a person, even a physically strong man like Gavin.

Clearing her thoughts, her out-of-the-ballpark concerns, she grinned. "I hope you don't mind the surprises, because I can't promise you they'll stop anytime soon."

"I don't hate them. Which is another surprise." Another deep, intent once-over before he walked to the beat-up coffee table on the opposite side of the room and deposited the pizza and to-go bag. Gesturing toward the equally beat-up couch, he said, "We'll eat out here. The kitchen is a wreck. I'll be right back with some glasses, plates. Just...ah...make yourself at home."

Haley nodded, waited until Gavin's form disappeared from view and groaned. Softly, of course, so he wouldn't hear, and then, because she had the very real concern her legs might just buckle beneath her, took a seat on the couch. And forced air in and out of her lungs.

Silly, to be so nervous. Unusual, as well.

Good, though. Being nervous about a man was *good*. Another couple of breaths and her heart stopped ramming so hard against her breastbone. She pulled in one more, for good measure, and stretched her neck to each side, to unkink the knots. Better. Definitely better.

Feeling more like herself, she gave in to her curiosity and appraised the living room. Like the kitchen, the room didn't boast much in the way of furniture: the well-worn sofa she sat on, the coffee table, one straight-backed chair on the other side, a card table in the far corner with a foldout chair and a laptop, and finally, a couple of floor lamps.

Here, she didn't see any signs of a renovation in progress, but she assumed a renovation would happen eventually. Probably after Gavin had completed the kitchen.

Large and rectangular in shape, the room extended the length of the house, and had wide, long, curtainless windows on both ends. Some type of wood—dark, rich, though in need of care—framed the walls and the windows. Avocado-green carpeting, ugly and threadbare in spots, covered the floor. Hardwood floors, she guessed, and without even asking, she knew one of the first things Gavin would do in this room was pull up that carpeting to discover what it hid.

Finally, she allowed herself to take in the true focal point of the room: the massive stone fireplace that sat in the center of the longest wall. Stones of myriad shapes, colors—pinks and grays and earth tones, in varying shades from light to dark—made up the formation. The hearth was large, also stone, and the mantel was likely cedar, though that was more of a guess based on her knowledge of other stone fireplaces in the area than a choice made with any surety.

Beautiful, though. Strong and everlasting.

A fireplace that all but begged people to sit around its hearth, warming their hands and feet, talking about their day, sharing their lives. A sigh born of longing escaped. Yes, this fireplace demanded attention. She hoped Gavin saw the beauty she saw, and that his intention was to refurbish, not to do away with or replace. That would be a shame.

For the first time, she wondered at Gavin's choice in purchasing this house, rather than something smaller, something that would require less work. Less of a commitment in time and money. Seemed awfully large for one man. Lonely, maybe, too. But in yet another way, this large and rambling house seemed exactly right for the man she was beginning to know.

Something else she'd ask. Later. Maybe not tonight, but at some point.

Her list of questions was growing by the day, rather than decreasing with each one she posed, and her curiosity about Gavin didn't seem quenchable. Didn't seem as if she could ever know enough about him, about what made him tick, or his past...or his dreams for the future.

What kissing him would be like, feel like.

Another soft, barely audible groan slipped from her lips. Butterflies reappeared in her stomach, her skin warmed and her mouth went dry.

All at the thought of kissing Gavin.

Twisting her hair around her finger, she stopped that thought process before it could go any further. If thinking about a mere kiss elicited such a strong physical response, what might follow that kiss would certainly be her undoing. Tonight was about dinner, conversation. Getting to know each other better. When—and if—a kiss happened, it wouldn't be tonight.

He wasn't wholly comfortable with her yet, that much was apparent. And...while she felt as if she'd known him forever, she hadn't. Even so, the idea of a kiss refused to dissipate. Her fingers went to her lips, and she was again lost in the image of Gavin's mouth on hers. Goose bumps erupted on her arms and she shivered—in pleasure, anticipation.

No, a kiss probably wouldn't happen tonight, for all the reasons—and more—she'd already considered. But why rule out the possibility quite so fast? The night was just getting started…anything could happen. Anything at all.

Even a kiss.

The first thing Gavin did when he entered the kitchen was try to find some peace, which entailed pacing the floor from one end of the room to the other and back again. Wasn't working. Wasn't helping him figure out any slice of what he felt, or what was in his head.

Not the happiness he'd experienced from finding Haley on his front porch, or the frustration that she hadn't alerted him to her plans. There was the reminiscent fear of wanting to believe in, trust, another person, and what the likely fall-out would be. In addition, as if he needed more confusion, he had this stupid hope in his head—his heart, too—that didn't seem to be going anywhere. Hope that strengthened whenever he heard from, thought of or saw Haley Foster.

Last, there was the guilt and resentment that the phone call from his mother had brought. His mother was in Denver, not in his living room waiting to share a pizza, which made it easier to focus on Haley. Easier, but no less complicated. Not by a long shot.

And okay, he could've sent Haley home. That would've been completely within his rights. She'd even given him permission to say no—not that he needed that permission, but still. That told him she would've been okay with a no, that he wouldn't have caused her any hurt or sadness by saying no, but when push came to shove, he'd wanted her to stay.

It was that simple, that complex, and that infuriated him, as well.

So here she was. Again. And all of this contradiction brewing inside was surely going to cause a heart attack. Or a stroke. Or…something. A man couldn't live like this, tied up in knots all the damn time. Over a woman. A feisty, impulsive, beautiful woman who seemed to have a heart made of gold and an undying belief in the goodness of others.

She would be hurt because of that belief someday.

And that right there, the possibility of Haley being hurt, brought his protective instincts to life with a roar, adding to the mix. When had he started to care enough to worry, to want to protect? Well, almost from the beginning. Before she'd trailed him up the driveway, he'd cared enough. He stopped pacing, admitted the truth again: yes, he cared.

Now what to do about that prickly state of affairs? He wished he knew, but she shouldn't be hurt. Ever. Maybe he could help her, teach her some of the lessons he'd learned. Course, she likely wouldn't listen, likely wouldn't see the sense or the wisdom in practicing caution.

A small grin appeared, easing some of his turmoil. Nope, Haley's mule-headedness wouldn't allow her to learn anything she didn't think she needed to learn. Well, then.

She'd declared them friends. If that declaration gave her the right to offer help he didn't want or need, to ask him one question after another and to stop by unannounced with a pizza and invite herself to dinner, then it certainly gave him the right to watch her back, to ascertain she didn't walk into trouble or trust the wrong person.

Sounded good to him. Reasonable. Something even she couldn't argue with.

For now, that had to be enough. Working out the rest of this wouldn't happen while Haley sat in the next room. He bent his head, brushed free as much of the dust as he could, did the same with his clothes. Next, he turned on the water faucet to full blast and washed his face, hands and arms. Really, he needed a shower. A change of clothes. And dammit, he still hadn't shaved. Irritated all over again, he grabbed the dish towel and dried himself off.

Why was he having girlish worries about his appearance?

Well…because he'd have liked to be better prepared. In addition to the shower and clean clothes, he definitely would've gone over those ideas of his for topics of conversation, so he wouldn't be so tongue-tied, flustered around her. None of this should be so difficult, he knew. Wasn't for most people.

Having a conversation with another person shouldn't send him spinning so hard. Besides which, she wanted to be here, or she wouldn't have brought him dinner. Folks didn't tend to deliver food to folks they didn't like, didn't think well of.

If nothing else, he'd eat when he didn't have any words. That would give him a few seconds—or minutes, depending on how long he chewed—to consider his words before he said them. A pitiful plan, no doubt, but a doable one. And right now, doable was all he needed.

Relieved, if not pleased, with the solution, Gavin retrieved a couple of plates and glasses, silverware, and the paper towels. Hell, maybe he'd even ask a few of his own questions. He wouldn't mind knowing what her favorite Christmas memory was.

Right. He could do this.

Still tense, but less so than earlier, he returned to the living room. Haley waited on the sofa, looking for all the world like a person one hundred percent comfortable with herself, her surroundings…him. She was… Well, *glorious* was the only word that came to him in that particular moment. Not a term he used all that often, but it fit.

Tonight, she wore her hair long and loose and free, just as he'd yearned to see it before. Her eyes were sparkling and her lips were…not so much red as a subtle, warm shade of pink. A slightly darker hue than the blush of her cheeks. She wore simple clothes: a pair of jeans and a soft-looking pale green shirt that clung to her curves without being too tight.

Really, though, what made her glorious was that smile.

Never in his life had Gavin seen such a smile. Warm and

real and…well, sweet, he guessed, was appropriate. Saucy, too, though again, the use of such a description sent a rush of embarrassment straight at him. How in heaven's name had this woman seen anything in him to pique her interest enough to email, bring him dinner, ask him questions?

Or, for that matter, sit in his living room with a saucy smile?

Those thoughts swirled and spun, mucking up whatever ease he'd momentarily found before laying eyes on her again. He opened his mouth, set to say something, anything, but that stupid cat came out of nowhere to cling to his tongue.

Swallowing hard, he forced his body to move in Haley's direction before she noticed his awkwardness. Or worse, commented on his awkwardness. Or worse yet, noticed without comment, but showed some sign that made him aware she'd noticed.

Lord, he was a mess.

Rattled. Confused. Unshaven. Yup, a mess, and in that second, what he needed the most was to know what motivated Haley Foster to behave in the way she did.

"Why'd you come over here tonight, Haley?" he blurted the question without proper consideration. Her eyes widened and she blinked, and regret simmered inside. He tried to fix it by saying, "That was rude, and not really what I meant to say. I just—"

"It was an impulsive decision," she said quickly. There was something else there, too. Some unknown emotion he couldn't put his finger on. Blinking again, she dipped her chin and stared at the floor. "I'm sorry, Gavin. I barged in again and—" suddenly, she stood, smoothed her jeans with her hands and shrugged "—I should leave. You're busy and…I should leave."

Narrowing his eyes, he looked at her hard, and recognized

what he couldn't before. For a beat, he was dumbfounded by the realization. *She* was nervous. And he'd made her feel bad.

The first gave him confidence, because if she fought with nerves, then he didn't feel so strange about his ongoing battle. The second made him want to kick himself.

"No, I don't want you to leave. In fact," he said with a smile he didn't have to fake, "I was getting hungry when you knocked on my door. And I'd rather eat with you than…well, just about anyone else, I'd reckon. Please stay."

"Is that so?" she asked, her voice faint. "More than anyone else? Really?"

"That's so."

The pink in her cheeks warmed to a rosier, sultrier shade. Her smile returned. "I'd rather eat with you than anyone else, as well. Or, for that matter, do just about anything with you than with anyone else. In case you're curious."

And didn't that just knock the air clean out of his lungs? Without giving himself a chance to second-guess a damn thing, he went to the sofa, sat down, patted the cushion she'd vacated. "Then I'd say we're both where we're supposed to be tonight. Let's eat."

She retook her seat, and they dug into the pizza. He poured them sodas, she doled out the chips. And for a while, they ate in silence. It wasn't awkward or uncomfortable. He didn't feel the need to fill the quiet. They just existed in the same space comfortably, without the tension he typically experienced with others.

Enjoyable. Relaxing. And, again, far easier than he'd have imagined.

They talked some, naturally, while they ate. About the house, the renovations—though he didn't mention his future plans, hopes—his job at the hardware store, her job with her family's businesses, and other odds and ends. None of which were particularly significant, but the conversation flowed and ebbed without so much as a hiccup…without Gavin getting stuck in his head even once. He didn't quite understand how or why, not in any way whatsoever, but he was beginning to accept that there was something different about Haley.

Something different about him when he was with Haley.

When they finished eating, she tidied the mess on the coffee table, stacking her plate on top of his. "I really am sorry for barging in tonight," she said. "And I wish I could promise I'll never do so again, but I probably will. No use pretending otherwise, even to myself."

He started to say that was fine, that he'd adjust, but stopped. Thought about her words some, about what made him comfortable and what didn't. Decided that if they were going to move forward in any fashion at all, he should be as honest with her as she was being with him.

"I can handle that…every so often," he said carefully. "But I tend to do better with advance notice. I have a lot going on around here, a lot I want to get done. And…well, I guess I like to plan, like to know what's coming, as much as I can." He fidgeted, uncomfortable with the admittance, with the worry that he might hurt her feelings. "I'm just not that spontaneous of a guy, Haley. So, a few parameters would help on my end."

"Of course," she said. Her eyes were serious. Maybe even a little sad. "I hope I haven't made you too uncomfortable. I just… I am spontaneous and impulsive, and sometimes I get an idea and I can't let it go. I'm not really a plan-out-every-minute-of-every-day type of person."

"Why not?" he asked, genuinely wanting to know. To understand not just her opinion on this topic, but her. He wanted to understand *her*. "When you have a plan, you can mostly be sure of what's coming your way. It's logical, to live that way."

Safer, too. A hell of a lot safer.

"Hmm. Good question." She twisted her fingers in her lap, and he again had the stunning realization that she was nervous. He didn't want her to be nervous. "It isn't as if I don't plan anything. I do. My workdays and big, important decisions. But I don't try to prepare for the moments in between." Lifting her shoulders in a small shrug, she said, "I guess I think that too much preparation can blind you to other possibilities. I would hate for that to happen. I would hate to miss out on something great."

Gavin weighed her explanation with his own beliefs, experiences. As a kid, he couldn't plan, control, prepare for, one damn minute of anything most days. Some nights, he'd go to sleep in one house, in one bed, and the next night he was somewhere else. So, while he understood her perspective, it wasn't his. Would never be his.

He considered, briefly, sharing this portion of his past, so she could understand *his* perspective. Decided not to. Seemed too soon. Doing so wouldn't be pleasant and would likely lead to other areas he wasn't ready to discuss. But no, he couldn't imagine living without a plan of some sort in place. Even in the "in between" moments.

"Something great, huh?" he said. "That sounds nice, but spontaneity doesn't necessarily equal good. Not being prepared can get you hurt. Leave you in a bad place, wondering how in the hell you got there."

"That's a point," she agreed readily enough. "But spontaneity doesn't necessarily equal bad, either. Anything can happen. And the law of averages alone will guarantee that some of what happens will be good."

Again, he took this in, thought about what it meant. He required structure, probably more than most folks. Haley didn't require structure, or at least, not as much as most folks. And this…well, it magnified the core difference between them. They weren't just opposites. They were oil and water. Tomato soup and peanut butter. One just did not go with the other.

As little as a week or so ago, this concept would've given

him relief. A reason not to bother answering her emails, her questions. A reason not to push out of his comfort zone. Hell, if he were smart, he'd end whatever was brewing between them. Now. Before someone got hurt. Her. Him. Would be easier now than later, he knew. It was the logical choice.

He always went with the logical choice.

Haley cleared her throat. "You know, even if you plan out each second of every day for the rest of your life, the unexpected will happen. Always does. Some good, and yes, some bad." She lifted her shoulders in a slight shrug. "You can't wipe out that aspect of life. No matter how hard you try. And I…I would just rather be optimistic and open."

Optimistic and open, huh? Scary way to live, to think. The open part, anyway. Maybe too scary for a man like him. "I think," he said slowly, "that we live in two different worlds, Haley. And I'm not altogether sure—"

"Stop," she said. "Don't say what I think you're going to say."

So, he stopped. Considered the logic. Considered his gut. And dammit all, for perhaps the first time ever that he could recall, he didn't—couldn't—wholly trust in the logic. Not when balanced with the comfort and ease that existed between him and Haley. Not with the way she made him feel when he looked into her eyes.

Well. He supposed he'd have to think about that some, too.

Forcing his body to relax, muscle by muscle, he took a mental step forward, and in a purposefully cheerful voice, said, "Not sure what you're thinking, but all I was going to say is that I'm not altogether sure we'll ever agree on this topic." Okay. That hadn't killed him. "I think we should agree to disagree, but respect each other in this regard."

She exhaled, squeezed her eyes shut for a millisecond. "Absolutely." And then she gave him a sneaky type of grin, and he knew they weren't done with this conversation. "Let me ask you this, though. Were you prepared for my offer of help at the Beanery that Saturday?"

"Nope," he said. Yup, she had a sneaky side, too, along with all those other irritating, fascinating qualities of hers. "Can't say that I was."

"Of course not. How could you be, right?" Brows arched, grin wide, she continued with, "What about when I followed you home?"

Hiding his amusement, which had come up from nowhere, he pretended to give the question due consideration. "Well, see, that one's a bit tricky. I wasn't prepared for you, specifically, to follow me home. However, beautiful women have a habit of trailing me…not just to my home, mind you. To the grocery store, work, wherever. So, I suppose I wasn't completely shocked to see you pulling into my driveway."

Wrinkling her nose, she said, "Beautiful women follow you around, do they? Well, isn't that—" She broke off, sucked in a breath. "Why, Gavin Daugherty, you just gave me a compliment. In a roundabout way."

"Did I?" he asked, feigning innocence.

She worked her jaw a bit before asking, "Didn't you?"

He should say outright what he'd hinted at, he knew. Just wasn't so sure his mouth could form the words and expel them. But he had to try. Had to find a way, so she had no doubts. "Yes, I did," he said. "I…can't be the only man who's ever told you that you're beautiful."

"You're not. But you're the first man I've ever believed."

"You should believe me. It's true."

Everything—the air, him, her—stilled. Hell, if he didn't know such a thing was impossible, he'd have believed that time itself had stopped moving. Within these seconds, the energy between them shifted, altered, and the connection— *their* connection—strengthened.

And a small chunk of his hard-earned shield, his protection—what he used to survive, day in and day out—dissolved into dust. As if it had never existed in the first place.

"So, um, where were we?" she asked, her voice soft. Whispery.

He pulled his mind back, picked up where they'd dropped the conversation and said, "I believe you were hell-bent on convincing me that being prepared isn't the be-all and end-all."

"Right. Okay. So, were you prepared when I—"

"No," he interjected. "I have not been prepared for any one action you've taken since that day at the Beanery. Nothing you've said, either."

Ever so lightly, she laid her hand on his knee and leaned in, so their faces were mere inches apart. His heart jumped to his throat and then dived to his stomach and then crawled back into its proper place, where it thudded hard and fast.

"Then I've proven my side of the argument," she said in that same almost-a-whisper, feathery tone. "Because there you were, adhering to your plans for the day, and there I was. And if I hadn't seen a possibility, been open to that possibility, I wouldn't have stepped behind you in line. I wouldn't have done any of the things I've done. And I wouldn't be here now."

Between those words, her touch and her close proximity, the control he'd only had a tenuous lock on to begin with also dissolved, fell away. He stopped worrying about oil and water. Stopped considering every one of the danger signs. The only thing he wanted—all he could think of—was pulling this woman even closer, holding her, kissing her.

Claiming her as his.

He had to kiss her. Didn't see any way around it, really. Not with her being so glorious and all.

Lifting his hand, he skimmed his palm along her cheek, rubbed his thumb over her bottom lip. The soft skin throbbed beneath his touch, grew warmer, and she moaned. A tiny, breathy, exquisite sliver of a sound that just about did him the rest of the way in.

"My intention is to kiss you," he said, meeting his gaze with hers. There, in the depths of her willow-green eyes, he saw heat, passion, desire. Want. *For him.* Amazing. "So, if kissing me is not one of those possibilities you're open to, you better let me know. Sooner rather than later."

She was there, then, on his lap and in his arms, before he'd even finished his sentence. Before he'd truly contemplated what kissing this woman would do to him. How it would change him. How it would change…everything. Too late now. Way too late to worry about logic.

He laced his fingers into her hair, brought his mouth down to hers and kissed her with the raw power of every emotion, every sensation, she'd ignited into being. Her lips were soft, tender, beneath his. Her hands were on his back, pushing him closer to her, and every now and then, another one of those tiny, breathy moans would escape.

She was, at once, sweet and spicy, strong and vulnerable, sexy and innocent. One kiss with Haley wouldn't be enough to satiate his craving for her. One kiss, one taste, would never, could never, be enough. Another chunk of his shield dropped away, ceased to exist, exposing his vulnerabilities. Exposing *him*.

This realization should have scared him, should have sent him running.

In this moment, though, with her in his arms, the scent of her all around him and the taste of her on his lips, he couldn't think about what this would mean tomorrow, or the next day, or ten days after that. Or hell, ten *years*. He just knew that one kiss wouldn't be enough.

Unexpected possibilities. Some good, some bad. He hadn't planned or prepared for this. Couldn't have seen this possibility on his horizon no matter how far or hard he'd searched.

Didn't yet know if this would prove good or bad or some-where in between.

But here it was. Here *she* was. And nothing would ever be the same again.

Chapter Seven

The next evening, Haley took the stairs from her apartment down to the restaurant's kitchen two steps at a time. She had this joyous energy tumbling through her veins, feeding her entire body with pure, unadulterated bliss. Even her upcoming dinner with Matt the teacher couldn't wipe away her good mood. Suzette knew the score, Matt hadn't really wanted to go to begin with, so she'd decided to put this dinner neatly into the "evening with friends" category.

It was *not* a date.

After last night's kiss with Gavin, she had a difficult time imagining dating any other man ever again. She wasn't surprised by this. Every reaction she'd had since meeting Gavin had risen above and beyond any of her prior experiences, including those of a romantic nature. Including kisses. She knew, whether sensible or not, whether anyone else would decree it possible or impossible, that she was falling hard and heavy and, knowing her, permanently.

That held some worry, because she didn't want to love a man who didn't love her for the rest of her life. In about every way she could think of, that would suck. Badly. But he'd made the move, not her, so that had to mean he was feeling some part or parcel of what she was.

Or so she hoped.

At the bottom of the stairs, she heard Reid's deep voice as he talked to someone, probably one of the cooks. Dylan, she knew, was working the bar that evening. Which meant two of her three brothers were on the premises. She'd be more comfortable facing Cole, as she rarely got anything past Reid and Dylan. They were like bloodhounds whenever she had a secret, nosing in and asking questions until they'd sniffed out the truth.

Well, Dylan especially. He seemed to know just by looking at her if she was keeping something to herself. Pausing, she composed her features, put Gavin out of her head—well, tried to, anyway—and inhaled a calming breath. If she waltzed in there brimming with gush, all bets would be off and her secret would be out of the bag. And she wasn't ready for that to happen.

So, she dimmed her smile, walked at a leisurely pace and entered the kitchen as if this were any other normal day and not the day after she'd had the most amazing kiss of her life.

"Hey there, big brother," she said to Reid, who was sitting at the table in the corner to the side of all the activity, enjoying a burger and fries. "Don't you ever eat at home?" she asked, falling into their normal, teasing banter. "What do you think this place is, a restaurant?"

He didn't respond, just winked at her as he dunked a French fry in a puddle of spicy mustard. She breathed easier. So far, so good. Mussing his dark hair with one hand, she moved past him to the small fridge the family and employees used and grabbed a bottle of water. Held it against her overly warm cheek and checked the wall clock. She'd gotten ready too fast.

She considered returning to her apartment, waiting out the remaining thirty-odd minutes there, but decided against it. Reid might not put any weight on a quick appearance-disappearance, but she was close to her brothers, enjoyed spending time with them. Under normal circumstances, she'd stay and chat, so why ask for trouble?

"So, Reid, I have some time to kill. Entertain me."

He rolled his eyes without comment and continued eating. If she'd said the same to either Cole or Dylan, they would've belted out a song or told a joke or picked her up and swung her around. Not Reid. Of all of her brothers, he was the most serious by far. He hadn't always been that way, but losing the love of his life—on what was supposed to be their wedding day, no less—had seemingly changed him forever.

Oh, he was still Haley's kind, sweet, loving brother. He was just quieter. More focused, she guessed. Intense. And he didn't seem to ever find or see the lighter moments in life. This saddened her. Confused her, too, since he'd never fully explained what had happened with Daisy. Whenever her name was brought up, he tended to change the subject. Fast. She'd long since learned to leave his past with his runaway bride alone.

"Talk to me," she said, hoping she sounded natural. "Or I'll be forced to resort to drastic measures to keep myself from dying of boredom. What's going on in your life lately?"

"Not a whole lot. Mostly working," he said, pushing his plate a few inches away from him. "It was a tough winter, so we're still dealing with cleanup and boundary maintenance. Especially in the tougher-to-reach areas. Have a few refresher courses coming up soon."

Reid was an equal partner in their family's businesses, and helped out whenever he could, but his actual career was as a professional ski patroller. He was less busy during the shoulder seasons—like now—but in peak season, he helped keep people safe. Rescued those who were injured, stuck, lost. And he saved lives. She was darn proud of him.

But she wished he smiled more. Similar to how she wished Gavin smiled more. Was there a greater connection? Had a woman broken Gavin's heart? Ugh. She hated that thought.

"What about you?" Reid asked.

"Ah. Pretty much the same as you," she said, her thoughts on Gavin.

"Same as me…what?" he asked drily, with a nuance of amusement. "Are you also maintaining boundaries and taking a few refresher courses?"

"No boundaries or classes. There just isn't a lot going on for me right now, either." She unscrewed the lid to her water bottle, screwed it back on and repeated the action twice more before realizing what she was doing. She ordered herself to stop thinking about Gavin. "Busy with work and hanging out with…friends. Watching books, reading movies… Wait, that's wrong. Watching movies and reading books. Oh, I painted my apartment a while back."

In a slow, methodical move, Reid lifted his napkin and wiped his mouth, eyeing her with curiosity. Balling the napkin, he tossed it on top of his plate. "You got weird there really fast. Everything okay? Anything you need to talk about?"

And there he went, being sweet and concerned, which flustered her all the more. Brought to mind how Gavin had asked after her when she'd trailed him home. "I'm fine, Reid. Promise."

"Then why the weirdness?"

"I believe you've mistaken excitement for weirdness," she deadpanned. Breathed in, and then out. "I know you don't see me excited often, so I understand your confusion."

"I've known you for your entire life, so I think I can say

with some assurance that you're excited far more often than you're not. And what you are now falls solidly into the weird zone."

"I wouldn't say that's an entirely factual statement." Excited, yes. Behaving oddly? Yes to that, too. But she wasn't about to verbally admit that to her brother. "I'm just happy a lot. Happiness and excitement aren't one and the same, but can easily be mistaken for each other."

"Typically," Reid pointed out, "those two emotions exist concurrently. But maybe I've misjudged what's going on. Tell me then, what has you so excited when, by your own admission, there isn't a lot happening right now?"

Oh, jeez. She should've seen that question coming. "Just that life in general is the same, but also, um…" She let her words die away, unable to find an explanation other than the truth.

"Exciting?" Reid filled in.

"Yes! Because, well, summer is almost here. And I love summer. So I'm looking forward to summer. Ready for the heat!" Well, okay. Her statement made little sense. Steamboat Springs had a fairly high elevation, and therefore was not known for its hot, balmy summers. Blinking, she gave herself a mental slap. To wake herself up. "Summer is…fun. Busy, but fun."

"Uh-huh." Brown eyes narrowed inquisitively. "You look nice in that dress."

"Thank you." Off went the water bottle cap. On went the water bottle cap. "Rachel gave me this dress, from her humongous designer wardrobe."

"Rachel's a sweetheart, all right."

"She is, isn't she?" Haley enthused, pleased they were headed in another direction. "And she'll make a great sister-in-law, don't you think? Cole's a very lucky guy. Do you know if they've settled on a wedding date yet? Christmas would be nice, since that's when Cole proposed. Such a romantic proposal! And—"

"Still being weird, Haley."

"Am not." She glanced at the clock. Really? Only eight minutes had passed? How was that even possible?

"Well, you are, but apparently you don't want to talk about it." Reid ran his hand over his jaw, gave her that partially concerned, partially amused look again. "You're okay?"

"I'm okay."

"That's good. You know I worry about you."

"You worry about all of us, Reid. That's sort of your self-mandated job as the eldest."

"I worry about you the most. Always have, since the day you were born."

True, she knew. Reid was seven years older. During her growing-up years, if their parents weren't able to attend a school function, or be home in the evening, or kiss a skinned knee, or calm her after a nightmare, Reid was there in their place. Almost always. As her caretaker and her brother.

She left her position by the fridge to give him a kiss on his cheek. "I love you like crazy. You know that, right? But I promise I'm totally fine. Better than fine."

He released a breath, pulled her in for a hug. "Love you like crazy, too." When they separated, he tugged a lock of her hair. "You're a little more dolled-up than usual, aren't you?"

"I'm meeting Suzette for dinner soon. Sort of like a girls' night out." Suzette *would* be in attendance. And two girls were enough, in her mind, to call it a girls' night out. "Nothing fancy."

Reid opened his mouth—to question her more, she was sure—when the door to the kitchen swung open. In came their mother, Margaret Foster, with an overly large tray balanced on one curvaceous hip and stacked dishes in the crook of her other arm. No one could carry the amount of dishes in one haul that she could, and Haley had tried…more than once.

"Mom," she said loudly. A little *too* loudly. "Let me help you with that."

"No, no. I'm fine," she said with a smile. "Oh, that's a pretty dress, dear. That's right, you have that date tonight, don't you? I'd almost forgotten."

"Aha! A date. I knew there was something going on," Reid said. "Who is he?"

"Hush, you," she said to her brother. Dang it all. When had she told her mother about the blind date? She went through the past few days, found nothing. Maybe her mother had finally learned how to read minds? Scary thought. "When did I tell you about this, Mom?"

"You didn't." Margaret rebalanced the tray on her hip before disappearing from view long enough to unload the dishes. When she returned, she said, "Suzette mentioned it last night when she called here looking for you. He's a teacher, right? Mark, Mike… Works with Suzette?"

Well, that would explain it. "Yes, a teacher. His name is Matt, but this isn't really a date."

"I don't know, Haley," Reid said. "It looks like a date, sounds like a date. From where I'm sitting, I'd have to call this a date. Matt who? What's his last name?"

"Oh, for heaven's sake! I haven't met him yet, so I have no idea what his last name is. This is a blind—" *No.* Not a date. "Um. A blind gathering-of-friends. For dinner. With Suzette and a couple of others. Matt is one of the others."

"A 'blind gathering-of-friends'? That isn't a real thing."

"It is so a real thing!" Now, anyway. "And how would you know? When's the last time you went out with anyone other than your buddies from work…or one of us?"

Dylan, of course, chose that second to join the bedlam. "Dad needs you, Mom."

"Well, of course he does," their mom said with a soft chuckle, making her way toward the door. "I need him, too. That's what makes marriage so lovely."

The second she left the kitchen, Reid said, "Hey, Dylan, have you ever heard of something called a 'blind gathering-of-friends'?"

"Um. No? Is that a trick question?" Dylan walked over and took the chair next to Reid. "That can't be a real thing, can it? Doesn't sound like a real thing to me."

"Yeah, I don't think it is, either. But Haley swears it is, and she's been behaving weirdly ever since she came down those stairs."

"Is that so? Weird in what way, exactly?"

Haley set aside the very real desire to clobber both of them over their heads, and instead tuned them out. Completely. Let them yammer on about whatever. She was blissful. Purely blissful, and even their annoying big-brother routines wouldn't drag her down. Not tonight, anyway. So, she waited them out while keeping track of the time.

They were, she decided for not the first time in her life, ridiculously handsome men. Cole, too, but he wasn't here at the moment, directly in her line of vision. Reid and Cole had inherited Paul Foster's darker-than-brown-but-not-all-the-way-black hair and rich, swoon-worthy—or so she'd been told by many of her friends—brown eyes. They were spitting images of their father, which also meant they looked like each other.

She and Dylan, on the other hand, took after their mother with their sometimes brown, sometimes auburn, sometimes somewhere-in-between hair—depending on how much time they'd spent in the sun—and honey-brown-to-sage-green eyes, depending on the intensity of their moods. All four siblings had the Foster build, though: tall, lean muscle and the ability to eat just about anything without gaining an ounce... or becoming ill.

Stomachs of steel, as their father liked to say.

Yes, her brothers were handsome men. Not as handsome as Gavin, though. Not even close. How she wished she was spending the evening with him, and not some teacher named Matt. Maybe, if dinner didn't go too long, she'd… No. She couldn't barge in again so quickly.

Gavin had made himself quite clear in that regard. She sighed, twisted a lock of hair around her finger. Sighed again. Thought about when she might see him, kiss him, next.

"I know what's wrong with her," Dylan said, his shocked voice breaking into her daydreams and forcing her out of her feigned indifference. "She has all the signs."

"What signs would those be?" Reid asked, again focusing his attention on Haley. "All I see is… Well, she's flushed, I guess. Seems jittery. Maybe she's coming down with the flu?"

"I am not ill," she said. "This is a kitchen, it's warm in here."

"Uh-huh." Dylan braced his elbows on the table, his jaw in his hands, and appraised her. "Warm in here, sure, but that doesn't explain the mooning eyes, your weirdness, or your unwillingness to admit you have a date tonight. Assuming, of course, that Reid is not behaving out of character and everything he's said is true."

"Oh, dear Lord. I think you're right," Reid murmured, apparently catching on to what Dylan was alluding to. "I don't have the energy for this."

"Both of you need to get a life, because really, there is nothing wrong with me! And there are no signs!" Another round of heat blasted her cheeks, radiated to her ears and neck. Nervous and frustrated, she fussed with her hair, wrapped her finger around some and twisted. "And what in the heck are 'mooning eyes,' anyway?"

"Dreamy," Dylan said.

"Dreamy?" Reid asked. "I was thinking more along the lines of vacant."

"Nah, vacant would be dull. Her eyes are bright, darker than normal. But bright. A bit hazy, too. As if her body is here but her head is somewhere else, which is why dreamy works."

"Er, I don't know. They look sort of stormy now."

"Well, that's because she's mad at us now," Dylan said. "But a second ago? Dreamy."

Reid expelled a loud breath, combed his fingers through his hair. "We could be wrong."

"No. We're not wrong," Dylan said somberly, barely hiding a laugh. "She's either fallen in love or is falling in love. Who's the date with again?"

"Matt. Some teacher who works with Suzette. But Haley said she hasn't met him yet."

Haley clamped her mouth shut. This was one of their tricks. They'd talk around her, as if she weren't even there, and inevitably, when she couldn't stand their annoying routine for another second, she'd let something slip. Nope, she would not respond. Would. Not. She'd done enough damage as it was. Far too late for any attempts at mitigation.

"Well, if that's true," Dylan said, "who's the guy?"

"Yup, that's the question." Reid closed his eyes, swore softly. Opening them again, he shook his head in a resigned manner. "Who is he, Haley? If not this teacher, then who? You might as well bring us into the loop now. We'll find out eventually, anyway."

"We will. We have ways of making you talk," Dylan said in a poor imitation of a German accent. Then, when she still didn't respond, he turned toward Reid. "Between you, me and Cole, we could start following her around. One of us could bunk at the apartment for a while."

He was teasing. Probably, he was teasing. But the threat alone was enough to push her over the edge. "I don't know what you're both going on about, but I don't have time to deal with your—your ridiculous, half-baked delusions right now," she said, waving the water bottle in front of her. "I have a—a blind gathering-of-friends to get to. And such a thing does exist!"

With that, she turned on her heel and strode for the back exit with as much dignity as she could pull together. Which, okay, wasn't all that much. Ignored the muffled laughter she recognized as Dylan's, the less-muffled curse she recognized as Reid's, opened, walked through and then slammed the door shut behind her.

Her brothers were onto her. Mostly, she knew, because of her epic inability to keep her emotions undercover. Two freaking weeks. She'd managed to go fourteen measly days without any interference. Was it enough? She reached her car and stomped her foot in a childish release of her frustration. She should've stayed in her apartment.

Too late to fix what was already done. Everything was about to get a heck of a lot stickier, because her brothers wouldn't let this drop. And Reid was right. Eventually, they'd figure out who had her all hot and bothered, and when they did...

Sighing, she stomped her foot again and let herself into her car. Sat for a minute, finished off her water and when there was nothing left to do, started the ignition. She'd have to warn Gavin. There really wasn't any other choice. She just hoped she'd be able to prepare him for the invasion of the Fosters. And that he'd somehow decide she was worth all the trouble.

She really, really hoped he'd decide that.

Chapter Eight

As Gavin walked toward Foster's Pub and Grill, he mentally went through his prepared speech. While working that day, he'd gotten it into his head to take a move from Haley's playbook and stop by, say hi. See if she might like to join him for a meal. Maybe even a movie. Chances were high she would, seeing how she liked to remain open to the possibilities.

Assuming she was free, of course.

And he wanted to try, wanted to discover how such a thing felt, and he wanted her to know that he'd listened to what she'd had to say on this topic. That he considered her opinion important. But that didn't make the doing effortless. Especially difficult since she lived upstairs from her family's restaurant—a fact he'd learned last night—so, unless she happened to be somewhere he could see her, he'd have to ask for her.

When he reached the restaurant, he found himself walking straight past the entrance, not quite ready to do what he'd decided to do. On his second pass, he did the same exact thing.

All in all, he traveled the entire block a total of three times—in both directions—before he was able to force his legs to stop at the door. Inhaled and pushed the door open, walked in.

Took a quick look around to situate himself, saw no sign of Haley. Lots of other folks, though, in the raised bar area and seated at the tables in the large room. Lots of activity and chatter. He relaxed a tad. In this case, lots of people were good. If the room were nearly empty, asking after Haley would be heard by just about everyone.

He'd still have asked, even though that would've been all sorts of awkward. This was better. Made him less self-conscious by a large margin.

Since he didn't want to take a table, he went directly to the bar. Stood at the end, somewhat to the side, and waited. Recognized one of Haley's brothers—Dylan, he thought his name was—and the senior Foster, Haley's father. Paul? Yes, his name was Paul. Well. Gavin would've preferred speaking to a nonfamily member, but he'd known this was a possibility. It was a family-owned business, after all.

Curious, he watched the men work behind the vintage, well-polished oak bar. The space behind the bar was long and somewhat narrow, but their movements were easy and effortless. They wove up and down, back and forth, keeping up a running commentary with each other and their customers. Sociable, charming, friendly. Exactly what every good bartender should be.

And while Gavin wasn't a huge fan of bars, or alcohol in general, he liked what he saw. Thought he'd probably like them, too.

Paul Foster caught his eye and approached with a genial smile. Wiping his hands on the white bar-rag looped over his belt, he said, "Welcome to Foster's. What can I get you? We have draft on special tonight, if you're a beer drinker."

"I am. Every so often," Gavin lied, returning the smile. "At the moment, though, I'm looking for Haley. She mentioned I might find her here, and—" he coughed to clear his throat "—well…I was wondering if she was around."

An assessing flash of curiosity entered the older man's brown eyes, but his smile didn't wane or falter. Nor did his friendly nature. "She was here earlier. Haven't seen hide nor hair of her in a while, though. Give me a minute, and I'll check. What's your name?"

"Gavin," Gavin said, reaching out to shake Paul's hand. "Gavin Daugherty."

"Well, it's good to meet you, Gavin," Paul replied. "I'm Paul, Haley's father, and any friend of hers is always welcome here." Then, pivoting slightly, he called out, "Son, do you know if your sister's in the back or upstairs? Or…mind running and checking for me?"

"Don't mind, but don't have to," Haley's brother responded as he pulled beer from the tap. "She had a date tonight. Left… oh, close to an hour ago, I'd say."

"There you have it," Paul said, facing Gavin again. "Not sure how late she'll be, but I can leave her a message. Tell her you stopped in or anything else you'd like."

Gavin nodded and tried to act normal. Tried not to show how staggered he was by the news that Haley was out on a date. "That would be fine," he said, keeping his voice even. "Just tell her I came by and we'll catch up later." And then, because he felt as if he needed to offer some type of a reason for his visit, said, "She had some ideas about promotional material for my business. I have a few follow-up questions, but I can easily send her an email."

"Our Haley is a real dynamo in that regard," Paul said, his fatherly pride evident in his tone and expression. The curiosity hadn't left his eyes, though. "I'll let her know to check her email. Guessing she'll be pleased. Can I get you a drink before you take off?"

Gavin pretended to give the offer a moment's consideration before shaking his head. "Not tonight, but thanks. It's… been a long day."

"Gotcha. Some days never seem to want to end." Paul moved down the bar to take care of a customer, saying over his shoulder, "Come back anytime."

"Will do." Gavin nodded again in farewell, and got the hell out of Dodge as quick as his legs could carry him. Well, without actually breaking into a run.

Once outside, he dragged in a lungful of air, shoved his thumbs into his pockets and headed toward where he'd parked his truck. A date didn't necessarily mean anything, he knew. Hell, they'd only been in each other's lives for two friggin' weeks. This "date" could've been set up well before that day at the Beanery. Well before he'd kissed her.

A kiss all on its own didn't necessarily mean a damn thing, either. From her perspective, anyway. From his, it had meant—still meant—a hell of a lot. He didn't go around kissing women just for the sake of kissing women. Or sharing why a memory held the significance it did. But they were different. Tomato soup and peanut butter different. So what meant something to him might amount to a hill of beans for her. A small hill, at that.

Even so, even with this logic in place, the idea of Haley being out with another man hurt. Probably far more than it should, considering all of the circumstances. Brought all of those doubts he'd barely pushed away right back to the surface. Made him question himself, what he'd believed might be happening with Haley, and… Yup, it hurt. Shouldn't, but did.

This, he decided when he reached his truck, was a very good reason to never barge in on someone. If he'd called her first, she'd have told him what was going on, or at a minimum, that she had plans for the evening and couldn't join him for a meal. He wouldn't have trudged over here with all these silly, old-fashioned romantic notions in his head. Wouldn't have left himself open to possibilities that likely weren't possibilities at all.

Also, though, he wouldn't be feeling as if a semi had just driven a path straight over his heart. And then circled around to finish the job.

Gavin fished his car keys from his pocket, annoyed by the idiotic comparison. His heart was fine. He was fine, would always be fine. Besides which, some folks did better on their own. *He* did better on his own, had known that fact for a damn long time.

There didn't seem to be any way of getting around that one.

Pleased she'd managed to sneak through the kitchen without being noticed, Haley climbed the stairs to her apartment. Thank goodness her "blind gathering-of-friends" excursion had come to an end. Using Reid's description, the entire dinner—from appetizers through dessert, and every minute in between—had fallen solidly into the weird zone.

Yes, Matt the teacher was a nice, intelligent and reasonably attractive guy. Not the man for her, even if Gavin wasn't in the picture, but she couldn't deny the accuracy of Suzette's description. Well, except for that whole "lack of chemistry" garbage.

Neither Suzette nor Matt had been able to keep their eyes off of each other for the entire evening. Neither paid attention to almost anything else that was being said, by Haley or Suzette's actual date—who was also a friendly, reasonably attractive guy. They laughed at inappropriate moments, fidgeted in their seats as if they both had ants in their pants, picked at their food, and when they did join in with the conversation, most of what they said didn't apply.

All in all, the evening had held an odd, somewhat uncomfortable energy. Whatever issue existed between Suzette and

Matt, Haley was fairly certain that it had zilch to do with a lack of chemistry. In fact, unless she'd completely misinterpreted the signs, Suzette was as crazy about Matt as he was about her, so why had she worked so freaking hard to set up this date?

Unfortunately, there hadn't been a moment of privacy during or after dinner to ask Suzette. Haley planned on calling her soon, though. Tomorrow or the next day.

Mentally exhausted if not physically, she reached the top of the stairs and saw that someone had left a Post-it stuck to her doorknob. She scowled, guessing Reid or Dylan had jotted her a note about her own weird behavior and hasty exit earlier that night.

"Dorks," she whispered, crumpling the note in one hand and unlocking the door with the other. Inside, she kicked off her shoes, dropped her purse and the unread Post-it on the table, and sighed in relief, happy to be home. Every one of her siblings had lived in this apartment at one time or another, but she'd been here for close to three years now.

The place was small. Her kitchenette wasn't large enough for a full-size range or refrigerator, and her living room barely held her love seat, television and bookshelf. Add in her bedroom, which fortunately had enough space to not feel overly cramped, the tiny-but-manageable bathroom, and she maybe had 500 square feet to call her own. For now, it was more than enough. And really, she couldn't ask for a better work commute.

Flipping on a lamp, she went to the bedroom. A hot bubble bath was first on her agenda, followed by a pair of comfy pajamas and then…then, she'd check her email. Maybe Gavin had written, and even if he hadn't, she'd write him before curling up with a book or finding something to watch. Just to…well, let him know she was thinking about him.

After soaking in the tub for a good hour or so, she returned to the kitchenette to grab something to drink and saw the crumpled-up Post-it. She should read it, she knew. The note might not be from her brothers, or even if it was, might not be about what had happened earlier. The message could be important. Maybe an employee had called off a shift tomorrow, and her parents needed Haley to fill in. Or perhaps a last-minute order needed to be made.

She stalked over to the table, picked up and straightened the wrinkled paper, recognized her father's small, almost pinched handwriting, and read:

> *A man named Gavin stopped in asking for you. Said he had a few questions and that he'd email. Hope you had fun tonight.*

Blinking, she read the note again. Gavin had come to see her? Wow. A warm fuzzy sensation enveloped her, wrapping tight around her like a cocoon. This…well, it was out of character for him, and that alone made the gesture far grander than if any other man had popped in unexpectedly. She let that sit for a minute, relishing how special this simple act made her feel.

Naturally, a slight fizzle of disappointment existed as well, since she hadn't been here to enjoy the moment firsthand. She wondered what questions he'd had. Wondered what, exactly, had propelled him to seek her out. And she wondered about what might have happened if she had been here, and not out for dinner. Another kiss, maybe?

Maybe that. She glanced at the note again, saw the bit about Gavin emailing her and flew to her bedroom. Retrieved her laptop, plugged it in and hit the power button. Realized another truth, one that kicked her nerves into overdrive. Really? Sometimes, life was unfair. Highly, highly unfair. Because if Gavin had spoken to her father, then Dylan had likely seen and heard the entire exchange. That would be enough, she knew, to raise his curiosity.

Particularly in combination with their exchange in the restaurant's kitchen. Knowing Dylan, he'd already phoned Reid to bring him up to speed. Alerting Cole wouldn't be far behind. Yeah, life could be ridiculously unfair. Haley breathed in deeply to calm her runaway thoughts, concerns. Her brothers weren't jerks. Not even close.

They were warm, compassionate, responsible men. So probably, their initial step would be to corner her, to ask her a bunch of questions in order to satisfy their curiosity and concerns. If she managed this conversation well, they'd step back and watch for the time being. Sounded simple enough, but if she failed to alleviate their concerns, they'd then take matters into their own hands to get whatever answers they felt they needed.

And this predicament right here is what worried her. She didn't want Gavin to be put in an uncomfortable situation, regardless of how well-meaning her brothers were. He wasn't a fan of surprises. He preferred to be prepared, to know what was coming his way.

Haley chewed on her bottom lip, glanced at the clock. Yes, she'd have to warn him, so he could be prepared. She could call him now. It wasn't that late yet. Or maybe she should wait until tomorrow, when she could try talking to him one-on-one.

After some thought, she decided to hand the reins over to Gavin. She'd send him an email, mention she'd like to talk— either in person or by phone—and go with whatever he chose. Settled with the decision, Haley logged in to her email program. Saw that he had, indeed, sent her a message, and in a snap, her warm fuzzies returned and her worries lessened.

She had a terrific, loving, supportive family. Gavin was a terrific man. They might have some hurdles to cross, but in the end, everything would work out however it was supposed to work out. And she believed that meant everything would be fine. Better than fine.

With her optimism restored, Haley smiled and clicked on Gavin's email. Scanned the letter. Her smile faded before she'd reached the end of what he'd written. Couldn't quite believe what she'd read, so went through the letter a second time, and a hollow, heavy ache began to build in her heart. On her third go-around, tears were filling her eyes. After her fourth read-through, she could no longer properly see, so she closed the email and pulled her knees to her chin. And cried. Softly, quietly, but for a long while.

He'd apologized for the kiss. He'd reiterated how busy he was. He'd said he didn't have time for distractions—even pleasant distractions—and how he thought it would be best to put their friendship on pause. Maybe later, down the road a ways, if life settled some, they could start over from scratch. But now…well, there were just too many other things that needed his attention. Finally, he'd wished her well. Apologized *again,* and that…well, that was that.

He was done. With her. With the connection she *knew* existed between them. With all of it, and frankly, none of what he'd written made a bit of sense. So yes, she cried.

When she was done with the crying, she went on to reasoning. Why had he made this decision? Because she didn't believe, not even for a second, the lame excuses he'd given her. Then, because she didn't believe, didn't—couldn't—understand, frustration roared in and she fumed. Also for a good, long while. After the crying, the reasoning and the fuming, she found her feet, her strength, and decided *she* wasn't done.

Not with him. Not with them. Not by a large margin.

If nothing else, she deserved a true explanation, delivered in person and not in a stupid email. When she had that explanation, assuming she even got that far, she'd appreciate the

FREE Merchandise is 'in the Cards' for you!

Dear Reader,

We're giving away FREE MERCHANDISE!

Seriously, we'd like to reward you for reading this novel by giving you **FREE MERCHANDISE** worth over $20. And no purchase is necessary!

You see the Jack of Hearts sticker above? Paste that sticker in the box on the Free Merchandise Voucher inside. Return the Voucher promptly...and we'll send you valuable Free Merchandise!

Thanks again for reading one of our novels—and enjoy your Free Merchandise with our compliments!

Pam Powers

Pam Powers

P.S. Look inside to see what Free Merchandise is **"in the cards"** for you!

HSE-FM-08/13

We'd like to send you two free books

to introduce you to the Harlequin® Special Edition series. These books are worth over $10, but they are yours to keep absolutely FREE! We'll even send you 2 wonderful surprise gifts. You can't lose!

REMEMBER: Your Free Merchandise, consisting of **2 Free Books** and **2 Free Gifts**, is worth over $20.00! No purchase is necessary, so please send for your Free Merchandise today.

Plus TWO FREE GIFTS!

We'll also send you two wonderful FREE GIFTS (worth about $10), in addition to your 2 Free Harlequin Special Edition books!

Visit us at:
www.ReaderService.com

opportunity to express her opinion on his reasoning. *That* was how friends behaved.

Mostly, though, she just knew she had to see him before giving up on him, on them. On what she believed they could someday be, if given the chance.

So, no. She wasn't done.

Like it or not, Gavin was going to receive another surprise visit. Between now and then, she had to determine what stance to take, what to say, how to get him to listen and not order her to leave, or carry her off of his property, or put their *relationship* on pause.

Really, she just needed him to listen. And okay, maybe to believe.

Gavin's mood bordered on foul for most of Sunday, though he managed to keep that under wraps and focused on his job, on stocking the shelves and helping whatever customers strolled into the hardware store. He'd made a mistake with Haley, he knew. If not in the decision itself, then in the handling of that decision. Cowardly, sending her an email.

Disrespectful, too. She'd gone out of her way to be nice to him, and he'd rewarded her outgoing nature by treating her poorly. Truth be told, he was ashamed by his behavior. He just wasn't quite sure how to fix the dilemma, or if a fix even existed. Or, he supposed, if trying to fix the error would serve any beneficial purpose whatsoever.

Probably not. There were many choices in Gavin's life he wished he could change. Numerous roads he'd taken where he wished he'd turned left instead of right, or vice versa. What had nearly happened in Aspen being one. There, at least, he'd done what was right. It had just taken Russ's letter to wake him up, to act on the choice he *knew* was right.

In the case of Haley Foster, however, he believed he'd made

the only decision he could comfortably live with. But the decision weighed on him nonetheless.

He owed her an apology. A personal apology, to boot, not another damn email. The thought of this—of looking her in the eyes and apologizing—tied him up in all sorts of knots. Seeing her again would… Well, it would make him want to do an about-face, take back his words, and he knew that would be another mistake.

Because he already cared too much.

Hearing about her date had hit him hard. Real hard. Logically, he knew she wouldn't have kissed him if she had romantic feelings for someone else. That just wasn't something Haley would do. Of this, he was certain. But dammit, he shouldn't have been—shouldn't still be—so distressed. So no, he couldn't alter his decision.

By the time he left work, he'd decided his best option was to call her. That way, he could apologize and still keep enough distance to stand by his decision. What he hadn't considered—and he really should've—was that Haley wouldn't sit idly by after receiving his email.

The second he turned into his driveway, every ounce of his determination skedaddled and his heart jumped around in his chest. Dammit all, there she was. Leaning against the trunk of her car, her arms angled over her chest and her foot tapping against the ground. Irked, without a doubt. Primed and ready to tear into his hide, most likely.

She'd earned that right, he reckoned, so he'd listen.

He pulled his truck as far to the side as he could, so she'd have room to back out when she'd had her say, and switched off the ignition. He brought to mind all of the valid reasons he couldn't allow himself to be swayed, regained his determination and exited the vehicle.

"Hey there, Haley," he said, going for casual. "I'm guessing I know why you're here."

"If your guess has to do with that asinine email you sent me, then you're on the right track," she said, scowling, her foot still tapping away. "And I don't care what you say or what excuses you give or how busy you might be, I'm not leaving until you hear me out."

"Fair enough." Yup, irked. Gloriously irked, at that. "I'll listen."

"You bet you will!" she said. "Because that email was rude and hurtful and…and…unfair. I happen to like you, Gavin Daugherty, and you kissed me! Two nights ago now, if memory serves." She stopped, gave him what could only be called a steely glare. "Do you recall kissing me? Or is that just some weird hallucination of mine?"

He swallowed, hard. "Not a hallucination, Haley. I clearly recall kissing you." A moment he would recall for however many years were still ahead of him.

Pushing off the car, she strode forward, stopping directly in front of him. She lifted her chin, planted her hands on her hips and said, "Am I a horrible kisser?"

"Wh-what? No. Of course not," he murmured, backing off a step. Just to put a little distance between them. "There's nothing wrong with your, um, kissing skills."

"Good. Nothing wrong with yours, either," she fired back. "But do you know what happens when a woman likes a man, that man kisses her and then, twenty-four hours after that kiss, that man has the audacity to end their relation—friendship via a freaking email?" She paused for maybe a millisecond. "That woman cries, Gavin. I cried."

"You cried?" he asked.

"Yes." She made the admittance quietly, but without even a hint of pride. "I cried. For quite a long while."

Dammit. She'd shed tears? Over him? He hadn't considered that his email would make her cry. Hadn't considered that at all. "I am very sorry to hear that," he said honestly, and he hoped she believed him. "Wasn't my intention and I dislike the idea of you crying for any reason."

"Well, as you can see, I've stopped crying." The green in her eyes darkened with temper as she stared up at him. Her lower lip trembled, and for some reason, that hit him hard, too. "And then I got mad. Real mad. And you know what I decided?"

"Mad makes sense." Far more sense than tears, especially tears shed over the likes of him. "What did you decide?"

Using her index finger, she lightly jabbed his chest. "That almost every word you wrote in that stupid email is ridiculous and untrue. You...apologized for kissing me!"

Wincing, inwardly as well as outwardly, he nodded. "Well, see, Haley, you were very clear in what you offered, and that was friendship. I don't typically kiss my friends."

"I'm a big girl, Gavin, and if I hadn't wanted to kiss you, I wouldn't have." She sniffed, jabbed him again. "I also have three brothers who have taught me how to take care of myself in prickly situations. Kissing you wasn't prickly or unwanted, so what is there to apologize for?"

Well, hell. "Because I shouldn't have kissed you."

"Oh, I believe you absolutely should have kissed me," she said with another slight lift of her chin. "And I'm very pleased you did. So, I would like you to rescind your apology."

"All right," he said, flustered as all get-out. "I take back my apology for kissing you."

A good deal of satisfaction entered her expression. "Good. Now, I would like to point out that life is busy. For pretty much everyone. So, I don't buy that as a logical, sensible reason to put our relationship—friendship, whatever you want to call it—on pause."

"Actually, it's quite logical." At her arched brow, he continued with the reasons he'd gone over, what he'd practiced. Hoped he was able to convince her. "There are only so many hours in the day. I have goals—very specific goals, and in order to accomplish those goals, I have to use every hour in the day to its fullest. Distractions hurt my forward progress."

"Hmm." Tap, tap, tap went her foot. "And I'm distracting you?"

"Yes."

"With two visits in two weeks and a few emails each day?"

"Yes," he repeated, without going into any further detail. She didn't need to know that his thoughts were frequently centered on her. She didn't need to know that the distraction she presented had zip to do with emails or visiting him. Had to do with *her*. Specifically.

"I don't believe you. What aren't you telling me?"

"I know I went about this the wrong way, and I'm sorry for sending that email," he said, skirting around her question. "I should have talked to you, told you how I felt, in person."

"Uh-huh. That would have been a good start," she said, her mad reappearing. "But you can talk to me now. I'm right here, Gavin. And you owe me an actual, honest, real explanation."

"I am very sorry," he repeated, "but there isn't anything else to say. My feelings haven't changed on this matter." Blinking rapidly, she nodded, and he prayed that she wouldn't start crying. He'd be on his knees if she did. "I…like you, too. More than I expected I would. And that kiss… Well, it was a mighty fine kiss. But we're not the same, Haley. In any way at all."

"Life would be boring if all folks were the same," she said softly, darting her gaze away from his. "Different doesn't mean bad or incompatible. Different isn't a reason to dump people you like, who you enjoy spending time with."

"I'm not, that is… I just don't want—" He broke off, unable to admit the truth. As much as he didn't want to hurt her, he was just as petrified of the damage she could do to him.

"You don't want what?"

"Doesn't matter," he said, harsher than intended. "I have… too much going on at the moment to devote any of my time to…anyone."

"But down the road a ways, when life settles some, you might have more time. That is what you wrote, right?"

"That's right." If the day ever came where he could look at her, think about her, without putting himself at risk or wanting the impossible, then maybe they could start over. He just didn't believe that day would ever come. Didn't see how he'd ever look at her and not want…more.

That was dangerous. Too dangerous.

"How long is this road, and how far down that road is 'a ways'?" she asked in a trembling, unsteady voice. "A week, a month, a year, ten? Or…never?"

Emotion clogged his throat. He ran his hands over his face, waited to be sure he could speak without the soppy brew leaking into his words. "I don't know about never, but…a while. I'd say a while. I guess if I were you, I wouldn't wait around for me."

Quiet descended for ten…twenty…thirty seconds. Pressing her fingers against her eyes, as if forcibly holding back her tears, she nodded again. When she spoke, she no longer sounded shaky. She sounded resolute. "Fortunately, I'm not you. Whatever I do next is my call."

No. She needed to leave this—and him—alone. "Don't go beating your head against a brick wall on my account. Trust me, you don't need the headache or the frustration."

Standing up on her tiptoes, she brushed her lips over his in a light, gentle caress that shot straight through him. Not so different from fire. Tempting, too tempting, to have her so close. Somehow, he found the strength to stand still. To not reach for her.

Right before she stepped away, she whispered, "I believe I've mentioned my tenacity, how I don't give up easily when someone matters to me. You might not understand this, and you might not even believe me yet, but, Gavin, you matter. One of these days, I'll find a way to prove that to you. One of these days, you'll believe me."

Every muscle in his body froze as he watched her get into her car, as she pulled out of the driveway and onto the road. As she drove away. No, this wasn't over. Haley wouldn't allow this to be over, and he… Well, for him, he needed this to be done. Finished.

Before he ended up worse off. Because he would, without a doubt, end up worse off.

And he had a gut-sinking suspicion that he'd never, for the rest of his life, recover once that day arrived. Hell, he was already wondering if he'd regain the balance he'd lost in the past few weeks. She'd already left her mark on him, had already changed him, had already shattered a good number of his barriers.

Well, he'd rebuild them. He'd done it before. He'd do it again.

This time, though, he'd ascertain that no one—not even a woman with a saucy smile and a heart made from gold and… and zero regard for boundaries—could break them down.

Chapter Nine

Early summer had arrived in Steamboat Springs, Colorado, and Haley's days were, once again, becoming hectic and long. Regrettably, neither the slowly warming weather nor the increasing surge of tourists had managed to relieve her of her misery.

She was still itchy. Still restless. Still waiting.

The only difference was that this time, she knew precisely what—or, in this case, *who*—she was waiting for. Day by day, her belief in Gavin, in them, in the hope that he would come to his senses and undo what he did, was starting to waver.

Ironically, all of her concerns about her brothers scaring off Gavin now seemed ludicrous. It seemed she had done a fine enough job of that all on her own, even if she had no comprehension of why, of what might have happened between the kiss and that blasted email.

Each day since that horrible, horrible night in his driveway, she'd sent him an email of her own. Just one a day, filled with basic, newsy chatter. She kept everything she wrote light, easy, in the hopes he'd eventually respond. So far, he hadn't.

Heck, as far she knew, he deleted each and every one without reading so much as a word. As far as she knew, he hadn't thought of her once in the past several weeks.

She, of course, hadn't stopped thinking about him. And she'd tried.

Antsy, Haley stood from her desk chair and stretched, and decided a coffee break was in order. She needed to work off some of this pent-up energy, and while they had plenty of coffee at the restaurant, she thought a walk to the Beanery would help in that regard.

She slipped out the back door, preferring not to engage in conversation with any of the customers or employees, or her family. While her brothers had stopped badgering her about her "mooning eyes," they and her parents had picked up on her current state of moping. They were concerned, naturally, and had taken to hovering in her general vicinity whenever they could.

She loved them. Of course she did. But sometimes, as Gavin kept right on saying, a person did better on her own. Right now, for Haley, was one of those times.

Mostly because pretending to be happy or cheerful didn't appeal, and she didn't much feel like offering an explanation to her concerned parents or brothers. She was still processing, she guessed, still attempting to find an explanation that made sense. Without this understanding, she didn't know how to proceed. Other than to wait and mope and send one email a day.

Being outside calmed her spirit, as it almost always did. She enjoyed the warmth of the sun on her shoulders, the touch of the breeze on her skin, the natural beauty all around her. And after being sequestered in her office for hours, the simple act of moving her body proved successful in easing some of her restlessness. She smiled here and there, to folks she passed on her path to the coffee shop. Said hi a time or two, as well.

When she arrived at the Beanery, she let herself in and glanced around the room. Most of the tables were filled, but the line was relatively short. Unlike the day she'd waited in line with Gavin and had confronted the standoffish woman. Unlike the day she'd been mesmerized by the mountain man, by his hair and eyes...by *him*. She gave herself a good, hard mental shake to clear her thoughts, the memory. She was here for coffee. Not for a stroll down memory lane.

The line moved quickly, and before she knew it, she was giving Lola her order. When Lola returned with Haley's iced mocha, the older woman's gaze narrowed. "You're looking a bit pale, sweetie. Coming down with something or just on the tired side today?"

"Oh, tired, I guess," Haley responded, handing Lola her credit card. "Midday slump."

"Well, the caffeine will give you a jolt, I'm sure," Lola said with a laid-back smile as she rang up the purchase. "By the way, Gavin was in here the other day, with more of those flyers. I take it that partnership idea of yours never got up and running?"

"He— What?" Finding her equilibrium, she shook her head. "No, that idea never went anywhere. So, ah, Gavin was in here, huh? How—how did he look? Did he seem happy?"

Heavily mascaraed lashes dipped in an exaggerated blink. "Well, I don't rightly know. He looked the same as before, I suppose. Though...now that I think back, he might have had the same tired, pinched and pale expression I noticed on you."

Taking that in, Haley nodded, and tried to convince herself that Gavin being tired didn't mean anything. Likely, he'd been working hard, filling up those precious hours of his to their fullest. Yeah, likely that. The possibility existed, though, that he'd appeared tired due to lack of sleep. She hadn't slept well lately. Too many thoughts of Gavin running amok in her head.

Feeling the weight of Lola's curious gaze, Haley forced a grin. "Well, I know he's been busy with getting everything up and running. I'm sure he's fine."

Lola snorted and slid Haley's credit card across the counter. "I'm sure he's fine, too. As fine as you, no doubt." Then, with a casual nod toward the far wall, she said, "He altered the flyer some. There's one on the bulletin board, if you're in the mind of seeing what he's done."

"Um, yeah. Think I'll take a look." Heart beating a mile a minute, legs wobbly and loose, Haley made her way across the room, still feeling the weight of Lola's gaze. She stopped in front of the bulletin board, searched for and located Gavin's flyer almost immediately.

Easy to recognize that he'd put some work into the visual appeal, to the layout itself. He'd added a few more lines of information, regarding equipment—he'd arrange for rentals, if necessary—as well as a more complete listing of his services and certifications, experience. It was a good, solid step up from the other flyer.

Now, if it were up to her, she'd add a photo of Gavin, maybe one or two shots of the area, trim some of the wordiness and print the flyer in color, on a glossy, heavier stock. The layout was solid, though, and she thought he'd done a darn good job. She turned to leave when an idea struck. Stopped and faced the bulletin board again. Stood there for a while, thinking.

Biting her bottom lip, she debated with herself, considered how much she just might irritate Gavin if she moved forward with her idea. Enough, possibly, that he'd seek her out to express his irritation. And no, her goal wasn't to upset him, but her emails weren't eliciting any response whatsoever. This... well, she thought this plan of hers would, if nothing else, put them in the same room. Allow her another opportunity to gain some understanding.

An understanding she desperately wanted.

Well, then. Decision made, Haley returned to the counter and waited in line once again. When she reached the front, she smiled at Lola. "Any chance that Gavin left more of those flyers with you? I'd like one or two, if so. Just for, um, informational purposes."

"Informational purposes, huh?" Lola asked, chuckling. "He did leave a handful for me to give to folks who might ask. Guess you fit in that category, since you're asking."

Five minutes later, Haley had two of Gavin's updated flyers tucked safely into her purse and she was on her way back to the restaurant. What she planned on shouldn't require too much time or effort to pull off. The end result might actually prove beneficial to Gavin's business. But that…well, that wouldn't matter since her plan also involved butting in where she wasn't wanted. The thought left her somewhat queasy. Didn't change her mind, though.

Something had to happen. And this was definitely something.

After she'd redesigned his flyers and spread them around town, once he'd realized what she'd done, she fully expected that Gavin would be irritated enough to come looking for her. Irritated enough to push past this self-erected wall of his.

And then, after he let off whatever steam he'd built up, she'd try to get some answers.

Working hard, especially working hard outside, was Gavin's go-to fix for just about any ill that might be bothering him. So ever since the night Haley had driven off, Gavin had been hard at work. In the house. Outside on his property. At the hardware store. On his business. And yup, he'd accomplished a hell of a lot. More, actually, then he'd have thought possible in just over a month's time. What the hard work hadn't done was give him any amount of peace.

Sleep had been difficult to come by, as well.

That woman had dug in deep, and despite his attempts, despite working his butt off every waking minute of every damn day, he couldn't seem to shake her loose. Course, those emails of hers didn't help any, didn't do a darn thing except keep her front and center in his head. And now…now, she'd gone and made her move, and he was, at once, smoking mad and…and grateful, maybe even a little pleased. And those last two just made him madder.

At the moment, he was focusing all of his energies on the mad.

Well, that and the ugly green carpeting in the living room. He crouched in a corner and, using a pair of pliers, tugged a section of the carpet free from the tack strip. When the corner was complete, he moved a few inches down the wall and repeated his actions. Pulling up carpeting didn't rank high on Gavin's list of favorite tasks, but the somewhat slow, methodical work gave him a chance to think, to consider how to best handle this flyer situation.

Four days ago, he'd stopped in at the Beanery to check in with Lola, to discover if any of her customers had asked about the flyers he'd dropped off. He noticed right away that the one he'd created was no longer on the bulletin board, replaced by a…well, a better, more polished version of his. He knew, instantly and without a doubt, that Haley was responsible.

And now… Now, those flyers of hers were all over the damn place.

Everywhere he went—even to his own job, for crying out loud—he'd see another. For the first few days, whenever he came across one, he'd replace it with one of his. But that stubborn woman began pulling the exact same maneuver on him. Since he didn't have the strength to engage in what could, and likely would, become a never-ending battle of wills, he'd stopped.

He'd almost stormed over to the bar to remind her of what she shouldn't need reminding of—that he didn't require her help, that he preferred to tend to his own business and that she needed to stop barging in, regardless of how good her intentions were. Luckily, his better sense kicked in and he'd managed to stick with his self-imposed no-contact rule.

Besides which, he figured she expected him to pay her a visit. Most folks would, either due to frustration or gratitude. And that was what had him all fired up today.

Her flyers had already brought in several queries from potential customers. Several more, as a matter of fact, than any of his advertising had. He had a few hiking trips scheduled for later in the week as a direct result, along with a couple of other possibilities.

If this kept up, he'd easily match his current salary at the hardware store. If it got any better on a consistent basis, he'd be able to quit his job there, which had been his plan—more like his hope, he supposed—from the beginning.

Good, yes. For his business and for his other goals, for getting the house and his property where they needed to be, so he could start the process of turning this place into a camp for foster kids and learning what would be required for that to happen.

To his way of thinking, all of this meant he owed Haley a thank-you. Really, though, wouldn't thanking her for something she shouldn't have done in the first place just spur her to do more of the same? And thanking her would still require putting himself in her presence. The entire situation had him this-close to yanking his hair out of his head.

Gavin yanked out another section of carpet instead, swore under his breath and, when that didn't relieve any of his tension, swore louder. But he kept thinking as he worked his way around the room, loosening every inch of carpet, as he began cutting the carpet into sections, and by the time he was finally pulling the carpeting free from the padding, he'd found a solution.

Chances were sky-high his solution would send Haley into another spitting-mad fit, but she'd started this friggin' mess, so he didn't allow himself to worry over that.

Much, anyway.

He hauled the discarded squares of carpeting to the bed of his truck to dispose of later. With that accomplished, he began lifting the carpet padding, being careful not to harm the hardwood floor—pine, he believed, wide-planked—beneath.

In an odd way, he almost wished he could see Haley's expression when she realized how he'd decided to handle this situation. Wondered briefly if she had another trick up her sleeve, some other scheme ready to go, or if she'd finally give up and go on about her life.

She should give up, in his opinion. For both of their sakes.

Heavy and sad, missing a woman he had no right to miss, Gavin stopped what he was doing and closed his eyes. Fought with the very real desire to get into his truck, drive over to Foster's and ask—no, beg—Haley for another chance...for her friendship, if nothing else.

He was still sitting there, still mulling over the idea, still trying to convince himself he'd made the right choice—the only possible choice—when he heard a knock. Insistent and sharp and loud. Whoever was on his front porch, they were bound and determined to snag his attention.

"Idiot," he whispered as he pulled himself to his feet. "It isn't her. Can't be her."

Within the few seconds it took to cross the room, to approach the door, his brain turned to mush and he decided if Haley stood on his front porch, he'd stop fighting so hard. If she had chosen to visit him at the same moment he had been thinking of her, missing her, then he didn't see how he could do anything but let her in. Sometimes, a man had to know when to surrender.

He opened the door, almost believing he would indeed find Haley on the other side. Instead, he found the only other woman on the face of the earth who held the power to hurt him. Hell, destroy him. And this woman had done both on more than one occasion.

"Hello, Gavin," his mother said, her voice soft and tentative. "It's so good to see you."

Shocked, he stared at her. "What are you doing here?"

"I'm here because you live here, and I miss you. And you won't talk to me whenever I call." Her eyes, a bluer shade than Gavin's, were steady and serious. "I'm not expecting you to welcome me with open arms. But I'm here now, for a while. I've found a studio apartment in the center of town. One of those short-term rentals."

Good. She wasn't planning on staying in his house. He'd have let her, because despite everything else, Vanessa Daugherty remained his mother. But for the few days or week or however long she'd be around, having her in his home would've caused far too much discomfort.

"You shouldn't have come here," he said, coolly and matter-of-factly.

"Probably not, but here I am." Her chin lifted in stubbornness, reminding him of Haley, and that grated. These two women were nothing alike. "Will you invite me in?"

"Don't think I will. Not today." Now that his shock was wearing off some, he took a harder look at her. She was slender, as always, but not bone-frail thin. Her eyes were clear and bright, her complexion smooth, and he hadn't noticed any slurring through her little speech there. All of which seemed positive. Even so, he had to ask, "You're still sober, I take it?"

"Have been for over three years now, Gavin." Sighing, she

ruffled her fingers through her shoulder-length brown hair. "I haven't had a drink for closer to four."

Longest she'd ever gone, to his knowledge. By a good two years or so. Didn't matter. Too late for them to repair anything, but he was…glad for her, hoped the status quo remained. He didn't say any of this, of course. No reason to give hope where there was none.

What he did say, all he could say, was, "That sounds healthy."

"I think so, and—" She darted her gaze away from his and a slight tremble shook her shoulders. "I understand why it's difficult for you to believe I've finally done what I promised I'd do for so long. I understand, too, that forgiving me for all of my…mistakes might never happen. I just want the chance to prove myself."

Her words, her tone, were all sincere and heartfelt. But they always were, every time she said them. Had she thought about him at all throughout those years, when he was being shuffled from one foster home to the next? Or how, at six years old, he'd already learned to hold her head in such a way that she wouldn't choke on her own vomit?

If she had, if she'd ever considered the damage she had done to him, she'd never said so. Nope, what his mother did was clump all of those messy little details together into neat, sterile, nonspecific terms and phrases. They were always her "mistakes," and "bad years" and "slipups." But Gavin remembered the messy details. Every damn one of them.

"I can't have this conversation now," he said in a measured, calm manner. Inside, though, he hurt. From the memories, yes. Also, though, from the echoes of the little boy he'd once been. A boy who'd loved his mother, who'd wanted nothing more than for her to love him enough to get better. And stay better. "How long are you in the area?"

"I've paid for three months." She reached into her purse

and pulled out an envelope, which she then handed over. "The address is in there. I'll be there—here—when you're ready."

Three *months?* "And if that doesn't happen? If I'm never ready?"

"I'll keep waiting." Tears filled her eyes. "And I'll let you decide when—if—you're ready to talk without any interference on my end. I love you, Gavin." Without pausing to see if he'd return the endearment, she pivoted on her heel and stepped off the porch.

Feeling as if he'd just taken multiple one-two punches to the head, Gavin shut the front door. For the past several years, he'd steered far and wide from his mother. She'd always known how to reach him, where to find him, because that was the right—the responsible—way to behave. But she'd never before packed up her life to chase after him, even on a temporary basis. Not once. Now, though, she had. It was a change. Something different from before.

But was that reason enough to justify another chance? Maybe.

If he had the ability, the strength, to accept the result, even if that meant a repeat of the past—then yes, maybe. But he didn't know that he did have the ability or the strength. Didn't know that he ever would. So, for now, the smartest action was to hold steady.

Folding the envelope from his mother in half, he shoved it into his back pocket and returned to the living room to finish the job he'd started. He had zero desire to look in the envelope, to learn where this short-term studio apartment was located. No reason to have that knowledge. At least, not unless he changed his mind.

Haley. He'd been way too close to giving in, to driving over there, to asking for her forgiveness and another chance. Ironic, that. Seeing how that was exactly what his mother had just done to him. This realization steeled his resolve, his determination. Yes, the smartest action on all fronts was to remain steady and unflinching.

With his mother, with Haley, with each and every choice he'd already made.

A check. He'd mailed her a freaking check?

Oh, and an off-the-shelf, generic, boring thank-you card. On which he'd written "For services rendered and costs accrued," and "I appreciate the time you put into this," followed by the scrawl of his signature. This was what her trouble had brought her?

Apparently so. Haley stared at the card and the check, frustration zipping in her blood. This was ridiculous and lame and…and…and, okay, damn smart. Gavin had outmaneuvered her maneuver, and he'd done so in such a way that she had no call to object.

Grinning in spite of her irritation, Haley folded the check in half and slipped it into the card, which she then put into her purse. She'd spent a full day distributing those damn flyers, and had then spent the next several redistributing those she'd noticed he'd taken down. All the while waiting and planning and anticipating the moment he'd seek her out.

Okay, then, that wasn't going to happen. She'd made her move, he'd made his. Now the ball was back in her court. Any additional attempts to bring him to her likely wouldn't work. She'd have to come up with something else. Something he couldn't ignore…or pay her for.

A glance at the clock informed her that she didn't have the time to figure out what that something might be. The workday was officially over, the restaurant was fully covered for the evening, and she had made plans with Suzette, whom she'd ignored for far too long.

After weeks of moping, strategizing and yes, waiting, Haley had finally decided enough was enough. No, she wasn't giving up on Gavin, even if she should, even if her optimism wasn't quite as strong. But she also wasn't going to sit around and just let life happen around her. So she'd phoned Suzette and invited her over for an evening of movies, junk food and girl time.

Maybe a few laughs as well, which always proved cathartic.

Haley set her desk to rights and powered down her PC, spent a few minutes chatting with her mother in the restaurant's kitchen and then climbed the stairs to her apartment.

He'd sent her a check. For services rendered and costs accrued.

Perhaps another woman would chalk up such a response as being a negative, proof that Gavin wanted absolutely nothing to do with her, and would then decide to stop beating her head against an immovable, solid brick wall. But Haley wasn't another woman. And she believed very few walls, whether formed from brick or not, were truly immovable.

Yes, she had expected Gavin to track her down out of irritation, annoyance. That was the predictable response, the stance that almost any other person would've taken. Since Gavin hadn't fallen into the predictable, and had, in fact, surprised her by his choice, she couldn't view his response as a negative. Instead, she felt oddly proud of him.

Other than her brothers, she'd never before met a man with the ability to accurately size her up, deduce her motivation and her end goal, and then conceive of a solution that was, at once, perfectly acceptable and seemingly final. Because, yes, most women would stop here.

Amusement bubbled inside and Haley laughed. No, this turn of events was not a negative in any way, shape or form. If anything, it refueled her hope.

Over the next several hours, her regained positivity didn't falter. Suzette arrived and, with plates filled with junk food, they piled on the love seat. By mutual agreement, they started their movie night with a tearjerker of a drama, deciding to get their tears out of the way first.

During their second movie, a romantic comedy neither had seen before, Suzette began to fidget. She went to the kitchenette for more junk food, went to the bathroom twice, and when she stood to go search the fridge for something to drink—even though she still had a mostly full bottle of water—Haley paused the movie.

"I'm not really enjoying this, and I haven't seen you in forever." Not since the weirder-than-weird date night, which Haley hadn't yet broached with Suzette. Now, she figured, would be a good time. "Let's chat instead."

Relief filtered into Suzette's expression. "You're right, this movie is lame. So," she said, clapping her hands together, "tell me about your mystery man."

"Actually, I was sort of hoping we could talk about Matt."

"Matt?" Suzette's gaze shimmied to the side of Haley's. "Why on earth would we talk about Matt when you have a new guy in your life?"

Haley started to relate her suspicions, but had second thoughts. She knew her friend well, and she thought she'd have to lead Suzette into this conversation with a little subtlety. Or better yet—if she could pull it off—some subtle *trickery*.

"Well, see, this is sort of embarrassing," Haley said slowly, working out what she wanted to say as she spoke. "But you were right, Suzette. Matt is nice and cute and smart and, from everything I saw, seems as if he could be the perfect guy for a woman like me."

"Really? I hadn't realized—" Suzette said, jerking her body to face Haley. "You think he's the perfect guy for you? After one solitary date, and not even a full date, just dinner?"

"I know, right? This is nuts, but that date was…well, unlike any other I've had. Ever."

Blinking, Suzette absorbed that information. "I… So you like Matt. Okay. You like Matt…. Wow," she said in a faint, faraway voice. "That is what you're saying, isn't it?"

"Yes, Suzette. I absolutely like Matt." Not a lie. Haley liked Matt just fine. She just didn't *like* like Matt. "But…I don't know if he likes me. Or if he's even thought about me since our date. Have you seen him recently? Has he mentioned me or asked about me?"

"Let me think." Suzette closed her eyes, gave her head the tiniest of shakes. "Um. Not really. Not that I'm remembering, anyway. But, you know, I could ask him about you. I… Wait a minute. When you said that he could be the perfect guy—" Opening her eyes, Suzette stared at Haley. "You're messing with me. This is one of your mind games, isn't it?"

"I don't play mind games. Now, sometimes, I'll use creative measures to help my friends." Haley donned an innocent smile. "Is that what you think I'm doing, Suze?"

A few seconds passed while Suzette appraised her. Then, flopping against the back of the love seat, she said, "You're a snot, for making me believe you like Matt. And I think you're far too smart for your—my—own good."

"I don't know about smart, just curious. Why would you set Matt up with me if you're interested in him?" Haley asked. "Because it seems rather clear that you are interested."

Suzette let out a breath. "Even if I managed to explain, I doubt you'll understand."

"Try me."

"Matt is sweet and funny and romantic," she said, flicking imaginary lint from her shorts. "And he's different from other guys. He's… I can see myself being with him for a long, long while. As in marriage and kids and the whole shebang. I can picture an entire life with him."

"I guess I don't understand, then. Because that sounds fairly wonderful to me."

"In some ways, sure. It's just…" She trailed off, returned to flicking at her shorts.

"Well, explain the other ways. What's the problem?"

"I just… I'm afraid," Suzette said. "This is new. I've never had to worry about a man crushing me." Looking up, she shrugged. "With how I feel for Matt, he could crush me, and that's frightening. So, I told him that it would be better for us to remain friends."

Aha. "And how did he take that?"

"Not very well. That's why I set you two up. So he'd believe me and stop pursuing me. And, as dumb as this is," Suzette said, "I really thought I wanted you two to click. Because then, the choice would be out of my hands. And maybe I'd be able to get over him."

Haley's mind whirled with Suzette's explanation. It was a foolish reason to make such a ridiculous decision. Shoving someone out of your life for no cause other than fear they'd someday hurt you did not compute. In *any* way. Why give up what was already good for the possibility of something bad? No, she didn't understand that mentality.

But… *Oh.* Was it possible that Gavin's equally ridiculous decision—and from her perspective, without understanding the whys, it was ridiculous—had evolved from the same type of mind-set? Maybe. Maybe not. But the idea stunned her, resonated with her and made her want to revisit every moment she'd spent with him, review every word spoken and every action taken.

"Don't live that way," she said to Suzette, her tone bordering on intense. "All that will accomplish is strangling the positive in favor of the negative. And leave you with regrets."

"What do you suggest I do, then?" she said with a small, strangled laugh. "Run over to his house and jump him?"

"You could do that," Haley said, smiling, "but you might want to start with an apology and an explanation. Tell him how you feel, why you backed off. And see how he responds."

"That would be difficult, but...maybe not entirely impossible." Suzette squeezed Haley's arm. "Thank you. For listening and for the advice."

"You're welcome. I hope this works out for you." Somehow, Haley believed it would. "Just don't ever set me up again. With anybody. Ever. For any reason."

"Deal. And I'm sorry about that...but hey, I still owe you a favor."

Bam. Just like that, another idea popped into Haley's brain. And this one...well, this was a good one. No way would Gavin see this coming...and yep, he'd be irritated. The possibilities, though, were too good to pass up. Because, assuming she managed to pull this off, she'd have an entire two days to spend with Gavin. Two full days. *Alone.*

"That's right! And I know exactly what I want that favor to be," Haley said. "First, though, I'll tell you about my... mystery man and why this favor is so important."

Forty-five minutes later, Suzette had all of the necessary information and had already sent her carefully worded query to Gavin's business email address. Once he replied, the rest of the details—the when and where—would be finalized.

And while Haley was excited about the possibilities, about the opportunity to understand, she also knew if this plan went south—which it very well could—she'd have no choice left but to admit defeat. Tenacity had seen her through a lot over the years, but stubbornness could only get you so far. If this failed, if this didn't give her the answers she needed and Gavin still refused to bend, then she'd stop. Any other step would have to come from him.

Which really meant there wouldn't be another step.

Chapter Ten

Squinting his eyes against the glare of the midmorning sun, Gavin leaned against his truck and waited for Suzette Solomon to arrive. There were several Routt National Forest campgrounds within easy driving distance from Steamboat Springs, this particular location being Gavin's first thought when he'd received the email from Suzette.

Admittedly, her request had jarred him some. She'd stated that she didn't have much experience in the great outdoors, but her boyfriend was a camping enthusiast. Since she preferred not to appear clueless to said boyfriend when they went camping together, she was looking for someone to teach her the basics. Her email had specifically mentioned fishing, raising a tent and building a campfire. And she wanted to hire Gavin for an entire weekend.

While he didn't know why she hadn't simply told her boyfriend the truth and have him teach her the basics, Gavin figured her money was as good as anyone else's. Swapping shifts with a couple of folks at the hardware store hadn't proved problematic, and once he'd confirmed the dates with Suzette, she'd agreed and mailed him a check with his full fee.

So, yup, a done deal. And other than his concern over making small talk, it was also a good deal. Odd, how he could easily share his knowledge about skiing, white-water rafting, hiking or in this case, camping, but had such difficulty with engaging in normal conversation.

Especially with strangers.

He just hoped this Suzette wasn't a squeamish, jumpy, socialite of a female who would scream at the sight of wildlife, freak out over a speck of dirt on her hands, retch when he taught her how to bait a hook or, for that matter, when she had to actually touch a fish.

Checking his watch, he frowned and searched the area again for the make, color and model of car she'd told him to keep watch for. Nope. No sign of her yet.

More to give himself something to pass the time than out of any real necessity, he hopped into the back of his truck and went through his equipment and supplies. He'd done the same earlier, knew without a doubt that everything was there, but another look wouldn't hurt anything. Besides which, he was antsy. Ready to get started.

He heard a vehicle pull into the parking spot next to him, glanced up, prepared to wave and greet the woman who'd hired him and…every damn thing stopped. Even, it seemed, the beat of his heart. Instead of the red Jeep Cherokee that supposedly belonged to Suzette Solomon, he saw a pale blue compact car with one Haley Foster behind the wheel.

Without question, he'd been had.

She exited the car with her trademark—read: glorious— smile in place and walked over to stand behind his truck. His heart started beating again, albeit in a faster, more jittery rhythm, and he couldn't quite decide if he wanted to hug her, kiss her or yell at her.

Maybe all three. And he didn't particularly care which order he did them in.

"Suzette Solomon, I take it?" he asked. "Because I assume this isn't a coincidence."

"Nope, this is most definitely not a coincidence." Haley flipped her long hair over her shoulder and narrowed her eyes in defiance. "I knew if I tried to hire you myself, you'd find a reason to say no. Suzette is a friend, so she hired you for me."

"Rather creative of you," he said evenly. "Especially with the whopper of a tale Suzette used to pull this off. But this isn't happening. You should get back in your car and drive home."

He stared at her, she stared at him, and again he was faced with a host of contradictory emotions. Keeping a woman at arm's length shouldn't pose so many difficulties. Course, he reminded himself, he wasn't dealing with the typical female. This was Haley.

A woman who defied every rule of logic he'd ever learned.

"Sorry," she said after a moment's pause. "I have zero plans of driving home."

"Well, then," he said, going for nonchalance. "Enjoy yourself. I won't be staying."

She huffed. "The only thing that's changed here is my presence, rather than Suzette's. Your job remains the same. Teach me how to fish, build a campfire and raise a tent. And, more to the point, you've already been paid. In full, I might add."

"Right," he said, latching onto the first argument that hit him, "because you didn't grow up with three older brothers who would've taught you all there is to know about camping by the time you were five. You could probably teach me a few things."

"Oh, they did. But I want *you* to teach me." She batted her eyelashes, widened her smile. "And I'm sure there are many, many things that you and I could teach each other."

Desperation crawled through his gut. No way, no how, would he survive an entire weekend with Haley. "You used my business in order to trick me, to get your way," he said as calmly as he could manage. "That right there isn't ethical."

"You've been paid," she repeated. "This is business."

"I'll refund your money."

"I won't accept another check, won't cash it, either." She stuck her nose up in the air. "Unless... I was thinking you need more of an online presence, some brochures and a few other odds and ends. I'll work on those, you'll pay me...and I'll just hire you again, using another friend as my cover. We can keep exchanging the same funds, for as long you like. Eventually, I'll have my weekend, Gavin. Now or later."

"You are not going to coerce me into this, Haley." Jumping off the truck, he planted himself directly in front of her. Immediately, he realized his error. He couldn't be this close to her without his brain cells malfunctioning, so he retreated a few inches. "There isn't one thing you can say that will get me to agree."

"You're wrong there." She crossed her arms in front of her. Still defiant. "I'm absolutely certain there is one thing I can say that will change your mind."

"Uh-huh," he said, mimicking her motion and crossing his arms over his chest, enjoying this—the moment and the woman—far more than he should. "If that's true, then why haven't you tossed this miracle statement my way?"

"Because I'd hoped you wouldn't put up such a fuss." A brief second passed where a shot of sadness, defeat, whispered into her features. He almost caved then, almost gave up the fight. *Almost.* But then, she pushed her fingers through her hair, straightened her shoulders, and resoluteness crept back into her voice. "I'd hoped you'd be happy to see me, in some form or fashion, and that we could have a pleasant weekend together."

"You tricked me," he repeated. "Hard to be happy to see someone when they pulled the wool over your eyes." He cursed himself, silently and instantly, for these words. Wool or no, seeing Haley did make him happy. Well…that and a slew of other emotions. Naming any of them seemed about as doable as breathing underwater. Sticking with his guns, he said, "I understand you put a lot of thought into this, but this weekend is not happening."

"Well, now hold on there," she said quickly, quietly. "You haven't heard my offer."

"And if I still say no, you'll turn around and leave?"

"Yes…for today, at least."

Her warning was clear. She'd leave, but tomorrow or the next day or the one after that, she'd pull something else. But those days weren't today. Nodding, he said, "Go on, then."

"Okay. Here goes." She inhaled a deep breath. "If you'll agree to this weekend, I…I'll stop with the tricks. I won't stop by your house. I won't even email you." The defeat resurfaced then. It was there, written all over her. In the catch of her voice, in the softening of her stance. Staring out at him from the depths of her soul. "I'll stop, Gavin. With everything."

A hard, impenetrable rock appeared in his throat, disrupting his ability to breathe. He'd wanted this, hadn't he? For her to throw in the towel and leave him alone, so she could get back to life. So he could…live within his barriers, without danger of them being torn down.

Yes. This was what he'd wanted. Or, he supposed, had convinced himself he'd wanted. But he didn't feel the slightest amount of relief. Couldn't feel relief. Not when seeing Haley this way—defeated and dejected and sad—tore him to shreds.

Haley Foster did not give up. She did not play by the rules or bend to anyone's will. This woman was feisty and impulsive and mule-headed and...enjoyed eating peanut butter sandwiches and tomato soup. She lived for the possibilities. Hell, she reveled in them.

Frustration percolated and bubbled in his veins. With her, for the tricks, the belief she insisted she had in him, in whatever she saw between them that made her charge through every stop sign he waved in her face. With himself, too, for whatever part he'd played in lowering her volume. Dimming the sun, regardless of his reasons, wasn't cool. Period.

"Dammit, Haley," he muttered, kicking at the ground with the toe of his boot. "I don't have one blasted idea of what to do with you."

"Oh, yes, you do. You know exactly what to do." Lifting her chin in that lovely, beautiful, stubborn-as-the-day-is-long way of hers, she said, "You're just too afraid to go there with me."

There it was again, that one-two punch straight to his skull. How did she do that? How did she see into his head—maybe even his heart—so friggin' easily?

"You win. One weekend." The words came out before he realized he'd made the decision. "This weekend."

"Told you I could change your mind," she said. "And I promise, I'll live up to my—"

"But your deal is off the table."

"Wh-what?"

"You heard me. This weekend, sure, but don't stop being you on anyone's account." Red-hot heat, prickly and scratchy, began developing on his neck. He tugged at his shirt collar. "That is the new deal. Take it or leave it."

"Um, wow." Pink flooded her cheeks, warming her complexion. "I'll take it."

"Good," he said before logic kicked in. "Get your stuff. We have a campsite to choose."

She didn't argue, but she didn't move, either. Not right off.

Rather, she continued to stare at him, her skin rosy and her hair billowing around her face from the wind. The moment didn't last long, but it felt…profound. Why exactly, Gavin didn't know. It just did.

"I have a question," she said, her tone now light and breezy and almost mischievous. A dangerous combination. "A very important question."

Ah. There she was, the real Haley. Thank God. "What's that?"

"I realized on the drive here that, in my excitement over seeing you, I accidentally left an item at home. A necessary item, I'm afraid."

Uh-oh. "What item might that be?"

"Well…I'm curious. Did you bring one tent or two?"

One. He'd brought a solitary tent—a small tent, at that—since Suzette had claimed she was bringing her own. So he could teach her how to raise *her* tent. God help him.

"You are, in every way imaginable, the most maddening woman I've ever met. And if you think—"

"I wouldn't describe you as calm and relaxing, either," she retorted. "Or any less maddening. Other than my brothers, no one has ever gotten under my skin the way you do." She blinked. "But just so I'm clear here—I don't think of you in a brotherly way."

Oh, yeah, and that did that nothing to ease his turmoil.

"Get your stuff, Haley," he said. "Before I call a halt to this entire fiasco."

She winked, grinned, but did as he asked and went to her trunk to retrieve her belongings.

One small tent and two people. Haley's body next to his, within reaching distance. Kissing distance. And the myriad other activities two people could do with each other in such a small, secluded space. Gavin raked his fingers through his hair and pushed those images into another hemisphere. Nope, he would not think about that until… Well, until night fell and he was forced to consider the ramifications.

And, he supposed, the possibilities.

"You didn't answer my question," Haley said when she'd returned with her duffel weighted against her shoulder. "One tent or two?"

"One," he said in a more of growl than any form of coherent speech. "We have one tent."

"Cozy and warm. Sounds perfect."

Gavin tossed Haley's bag into the truck, motioned for her to get in. And didn't say a damn word to either of her comments. Cozy and warm, huh? Those terms worked well enough, but he could think of quite a few others. Likely would think of them, basically nonstop, for the next two days. And while he lay awake at night, unable to sleep.

Nope, no way in hell was he surviving this weekend.

Restless and sleepy, Haley kept her vision glued to Gavin's charcoal-colored, flannel-shirt-covered back as they made their way to the lake. To fish. He'd shaken her awake this morning—far too early for any sane person to be forced to open their eyes—and stated she should get moving, so they could eat breakfast before embarking on their fishing expedition.

Why in heaven's name had she told Suzette to add fishing to the list?

Well, because she'd wanted Suzette's email to sound legit, and other than raising a tent and building a fire, she hadn't been able to conceive of another need-to-learn "basic" camping activity. So, fishing it was. But she'd rather be back in that tent, snug and warm and sleeping, than trudging along in the cold, foggy morning air.

It was a hideous way to the start the day.

On the plus side, she was with Gavin. *Finally.* On the negative, she hadn't yet made one single step of progress with him. She sniffed in annoyance. He hadn't so much as breathed in her direction last night, let alone actually touched her. Kissed her. Had his way with her.

Nope. That dratted man had stayed in his sleeping bag, back turned toward her, quiet and still. And she'd stayed in hers, frustrated beyond belief, unable to fall asleep for hours.

Sidestepping a fallen branch, Haley picked up her pace. The gray of his shirt was quickly merging with the gray of the morning, making it difficult to see him all that clearly. And he walked fast. Super-duper fast. Those long legs of his didn't help.

"Wait up, why don't you? Jeez," she called out, exasperated. "We're not in any rush, are we? And this isn't a race. And darn it, I could really use more coffee."

He stopped instantly, and waited for her to catch up. "Grouchy this morning," he said smoothly, almost humorously. "And you could have had more coffee if you'd gotten up faster."

"This is supposed to be a relaxing, pleasant weekend. Insisting I be cheerful and awake at the crack of dawn with only one cup of coffee consumed isn't relaxing or pleasant. Or nice."

"You didn't hire me to be nice." He started walking again, at a somewhat slower pace. She still had to speed-walk to keep up with him. "You hired me to teach you the basics of camping. Part of that, if I recall correctly, was fishing. Best time to fish is early in the morning."

So reasonable. So logical. So annoyingly distant.

She might just have to shove him in the lake. The thought amused her, lessened some of her grouchiness. Whatever breakthrough she'd believed they'd gained yesterday morning had faded some by the time they'd set up camp. As the day continued, he'd been the perfect guide and teacher, patiently and systematically explaining the how-tos on every single thing they did.

Which, okay, that was fine. Any talking was better than no talking, and really, for a while she'd been content enough to just be near him. But as afternoon became early evening, his distant behavior grew and he stopped talking pretty much altogether.

The whole point of this weekend—her sexual attraction toward Gavin notwithstanding—was to gain a better understanding of him, to learn what had happened to change their direction so quickly, and hopefully with this understanding, find a way to put them back on course.

He needed to talk to her, open up some, in order for that to happen.

Arriving at the lake, Gavin gestured for her to come nearer and then proceeded to demonstrate how to bait a hook. She watched and listened, because despite Gavin's guess that she'd grown up fishing, she hadn't. Her brothers and father fished. She and her mother did other, less disgusting, less smelly activities while the men fished.

And not one of them had involved handling a freaking worm.

"Okay, your turn," Gavin said, nodding toward the plastic container filled with dirt and squirming worms. "Pick one about twice the length of your hook, and then just do what I did."

"Right!" Grimacing, Haley pushed at the soil with the tip of her finger, trying to avoid actually touching a worm without making the avoidance obvious. "I prefer fishing with lures. Live bait seems…so cruel. To the worms. I mean, really, would you like to have a hook skewered through you—twice—and then have your body dangled into the water to be eaten?"

"Is that a serious question?" Gavin spoke in a dry, semi-sarcastic tenor that had Haley thinking, once again, about shoving him into the lake. Face-first.

"Yes, it is a serious question," she said. "Because I'm trying to demonstrate what these poor worms' lives are like, but if you're okay with killing innocent creatures that have done you no harm, all in the name of...of—" Oh. Okay, yeah, that argument wasn't going to fly.

"Catching innocent fish?" The corners of his mouth twitched. "Who have also done me no harm? And then... eating the fish?"

"Barbaric," she said, grinning for the first time that day. "But I guess I didn't totally think that through. My point, however, is that I prefer lures. Did you bring any with you?"

The blue in his eyes deepened as he laughed, and she thought she could stand right where they were, look into those gorgeous eyes of his and listen to him laugh all day. All night.

"Nope. No lures," he said with a wink and a grin. "You'll have to use the worm."

"I really, really don't want to...kill a worm. They're so—" she almost choked on the words, but managed to spit them out "—cute and...cuddly? Well, definitely not cute. And cuddly applies more to teddy bears than to anything that squirms. Do they deserve death, though?"

"But see, Haley, you don't actually kill the worm." He paused for a beat. "The fish does."

"Wow, Gavin, that totally helps," she said brightly. "Thanks for that bit of illuminating information. I feel so much better now about...touching and impaling a worm. So much better."

Gavin's gaze held hers steadily. "Dammit, Haley."

"Um, dammit? What—"

Before she could finish her sentence, before she even realized what was happening, Gavin dropped his fishing pole, tugged hers out of her grasp and dropped that, too. Pulled her to him and, for another beat, simply held her. And suddenly, she was very, very happy he'd insisted they wake up at the crack of dawn. Happy and optimistic and relieved.

So very relieved.

He tipped her chin up and looked into her eyes for a second, closed his for twice that and let out a long, deliberate sigh. His hands, rough and warm and delicious against her skin, came to her cheeks. Slowly—so freaking slowly she thought she might die from the wait—he brought his lips to hers and began kissing her. Her blood fizzed and popped, warmth and desire curled tight in her belly before saturating the rest of her in delectable heat.

She heard herself moan. Heard him moan in return.

Deepening the kiss, his mouth became hard and insistent, thorough and intense, begging—demanding, really—for her complete and undivided attention. All of this, the passion and desire and the feel of his mouth upon hers, melted her concerns and fears into nothingness, as if they'd never existed. Until all that remained was the same as what she'd started with, from almost the moment Gavin Daugherty had entered her life.

Hope. Belief. Absolute certainty that this man was an essential piece of her soul. And that she had to do whatever she could, whatever was in her power, to make him hers. Because she knew, more than she had before, that she'd been his all along.

Would always be his.

Gavin sighed a ragged, breathless sound. Kissed her along her chin, the curve of her cheekbones, and finally, her forehead. He rested his forehead against hers, kept her body tight to his, and…held her. As if she were the most precious cargo in the world.

"Dammit, Haley," he repeated, his voice gruff. "You had to go and do this, didn't you?"

"Do what?" she whispered, still lost in the moment. Still

tingling and hyperaware and...a good bit more centered. Whole. "And why do you keep saying 'dammit'?"

"Doesn't matter," he said. "Not anymore."

Well, she thought it likely did matter. Probably a heck of a lot. Arguing with him now, though, seemed counterproductive. He'd kissed her. They had the entire day and night before them. "Okay," she said easily, her body still pressed tight against his. "I like kissing you, Gavin."

"I like kissing you, too." Then, as if the admittance weighed too heavy to bear, he dropped his hold and stepped away. She missed him instantly. Picking up their fishing poles, he handed hers over and grinned. "Still need to bait your hook, Haley."

"Um. I... Well, that is, how about if I just watch you fish? A person can learn a lot by watching, you know. Sometimes more than doing, because—"

"Nah," he said, his grin wider. "I've found that doing is always the best way to learn." With that, Gavin reached into the plastic tub and pulled out a long, wiggly worm and held it in front of her. "It's just a worm, Haley. And this is easy. I know you can do it."

Those words, his belief in her—even over something as simple as this—propelled her forward. She sucked in a breath, took the worm and baited the hook as quickly as possible. And no, it wasn't that bad. But she wasn't in any hurry to do it again. "There, done. Now what?"

"Now, my dear, we fish."

Chapter Eleven

Shivering, Haley scooted closer to the snapping, spitting campfire while waiting for Gavin to return from his pickup, which was parked just out and down a bit from their campsite. He'd decided, after they'd eaten, to get an early start on loading the truck. Of course, this only included those items they wouldn't need before they left, but she supposed it made sense.

She just wasn't yet ready to think about morning, about leaving.

Between the kiss and the fishing—which, surprisingly, hadn't been awful—the rest of the day had progressed in an easier, more relaxed fashion than yesterday. After fishing for several hours, they'd packed a lunch and spent the afternoon hiking a few of the trails. They hadn't kissed again, which was a downright shame for many, many reasons, but they had held hands here and there, and their conversation hadn't fallen into the overly awkward or stilted range.

. All positive signs.

Except they hadn't discussed anything to do with them, or what would happen once they returned to Steamboat Springs tomorrow. So Haley was caught between wanting to believe they had turned a corner and an uncomfortable sense of surety that they really hadn't. They needed to talk, she knew. Needed to find a place of balance that would hopefully work for both of them.

Sighing, she pulled her long green sweater over her knees and considered how to begin this particular conversation. She feared Gavin would just walk away again if she pushed too hard. And she knew darn well that she often pushed too hard.

Sometimes due to her heart-on-sleeve tendencies. Other times, due to her desire to find solutions. And, of course, there were those times—fortunately, few and far between—where she wanted something the other person absolutely did not. In those cases, it really didn't matter how often or hard she smacked her head against that metaphorical brick wall. Because those were the times that stupid brick wall truly was immovable.

Making another person do, or be, or feel anything he did not want, or wasn't prepared to do, or be, or feel was, in pretty much all ways, an impossible feat.

She trusted her instincts, and they told her in no uncertain terms that this connection with Gavin was true. Real. Solid. She even believed that Gavin recognized their connection, as well. But that didn't mean they viewed the connection in the same manner, or even that their hopes—wants—were lined up with each other. They might not be.

And…well, that possibility sucked all of the wind right out of her sails. Scared her, too. She'd wait for one year, ten years, twenty…more if necessary, as long as they were on the same path, headed in the same direction. But if they weren't, if Gavin's wants didn't line up with hers in this regard, then she wouldn't—couldn't—spend her life hoping that would change.

That, she knew, would prove far too painful. That would be the brick wall she wouldn't be able to move. Not with any amount of trickery or impulsivity or stubbornness.

Haley twisted her finger around a lock of her hair, lost in thought. So, okay, this was what she needed to determine. She didn't want to fall completely head over heels if Gavin wasn't prepared or able to even try at a relationship.

Caught up as she was in her concerns, her emotions, she didn't hear Gavin's approach until he'd fully stepped into their campsite. She couldn't see him well in the dark, even with the glow from the campfire, but his physical presence warmed her from the inside out.

He walked over to the fire, on the other side from where she sat, and rubbed his hands above the flames. In a casual, almost offhand manner, he said, "If you don't have to be back too early tomorrow, I was thinking we could go on one more hike in the morning."

"Yes," she said, pleased he had the thought. More pleased that the thought had become an actual invitation. "I would enjoy a morning hike. Just, um, not too early. Okay?"

He laughed in that warm, rich way of his that always brought a smile to her lips. "You got it. I'll even allow two cups of coffee before we get started."

"Wow, how generous of you," she teased. "Though I will say if we ever do this again, we need better coffee than that instant stuff. Oh, and marshmallows and chocolate bars and graham crackers. I would love a s'more right now."

"S'mores are good. I haven't had one—" He stopped. Coughed. "It's been a long time."

"How long?"

"I was thirteen. At a campground not too far from here, actually."

"Really?" She knew so little about his past, other than the Christmas memory he'd shared. And she wanted to know more...yearned to know more. Patting the blanket she sat on, she said, "Sit with me, please. Did you go camping often as a kid?"

"Fairly often for a couple of years. Not so much before or after." As he spoke, he rounded the fire and sat next to her. "Most...well, most of the foster parents I lived with didn't do much with us kids. But there was that one couple I told you about. Russ and Elaine were great. Really great. They brought us to Steamboat Springs to ski in the winter and to hike, camp in the summer."

"How long did you live with them?" she asked, interested. Cautious, though, too. She sensed he didn't talk about his past often.

"Longer than I lived anywhere else," he said, his voice rough and scratchy. "Close to three years. Moved in when I was twelve, that August. Moved out the July after my third Christmas with them. One month shy of three years."

The knowledge that Gavin hadn't lived anywhere for longer than "close to three years" while growing up saddened her, made her realize how lucky she was for her family, to have been blessed with loving, stable parents. "Did you have to move out? I mean...I don't know a lot about the foster care system, so I'm curious."

"Russ's job relocated out of state. They couldn't take me with them. But I found out later, a few years ago now, that they'd wanted to adopt me. Tried to figure it out before they moved, but...well, it couldn't be done." Sadness echoed in his voice. Her heart cracked in two. "There was this other kid staying with us, Brett. They adopted him."

And now her heart smashed into bits. Haley reached for Gavin's hand, lacing her fingers through his, and squeezed. "I'm sorry. That...sucks. Was there a reason they were able to adopt Brett, but they weren't able to adopt you? If you don't mind telling me."

"Not much to say on this, really, so I don't mind." Even so, he paused, drew in a breath before continuing. "Brett was alone in the world, didn't have any living blood relatives, which made the process easier for Russ and Elaine."

Haley took this in, added two plus two. "So, you did have living blood relatives?"

"Yes. My mother." Now his voice was flat, emotionless. "Glad I didn't know this was all going on then. Was tough leaving them. But I guess I'm glad now. Russ…he died several years ago… There was a letter. Some money, too. But the letter explained what they'd tried to do, what they couldn't do. And…yeah, I'm glad I know now."

Closing her eyes, Haley breathed in the night air and attempted to find her balance. Attempted to understand a life so different from her own. "If—if your mom was around, why were you in foster care? What… I mean, why weren't you with her?"

She wanted to know. Wanted to learn as much about this man as possible. Because, yes, she wanted to know what made him tick. Also, though, she had the weird idea that if he talked about this, she could absorb some of his pain. Or maybe she could just carry it with him.

Initially, she didn't think he was going to answer. Thought perhaps she'd gone too far. She felt more than saw his body tense. And his hand tightened into a fist for a millisecond before relaxing again. Yes. This was hard for him.

He expelled a sigh. "My dad died when I was four. My mom had a real rough time after this. A lot of things changed, and she…I guess it's simplest to say she had difficulty caring for herself, and then later, difficulty caring for me. It… well, it got pretty bad."

Inching closer to Gavin, she rested her head on his arm.

"In what way?" she asked softly, her heart still in pieces, her soul aching for him, for the little boy he was. For the man, too. "What happened that put you in foster care?"

She sensed he was fighting with himself, for the words to use. Maybe for the will to say them. "She drank. My mother drank a lot. Took to leaving me alone. I... When I was seven, she disappeared for a couple of days. I... Well, she hadn't been gone for that long ever before and I got scared. Wasn't much food left in the place. Called the police."

Oh, God. Tears built behind Haley's eyes and it was all she could do not to sob. Fury, too, existed, for a woman with an unknown face. Unknown name. "And the police came, I'm guessing. Saw what was going on, put you into the state's custody."

"Yup."

"Did you...did you ever see her again? Your mom?"

"She cleaned up here and there. Long enough, a few times, to regain custody. Never lasted for long. Never—" He stopped, cursed. "I'm not trying to be rude here, and I've already said more than I meant. I... What's past is past. Don't much see the point in talking about this."

"Okay, that's fine. Of course it's fine." And it was. He'd shared more with her than he likely had before, she guessed. And she'd like to hear more, know more, for his sake, for hers. Someday, maybe he'd want her to know. Would want to talk more. Until then, "We can talk about something else. Or, we can just sit here and look at the fire."

His tension eased, which she again felt more than saw, and he began rubbing his thumb on her palm. "Either. I'm good with either. Though, there is something that I believe I'd like to tell you about. If... Well, maybe this isn't such a good—"

"Anything you want to share is a good idea," she interjected. "And I want to listen."

He cleared his throat once. Twice. "Well, see...when I told

you I didn't have time for distractions, I wasn't lying. I have a lot going on, Haley."

"So you've mentioned," she said, fearing they were walking right back into the place she'd worked so hard to get past. "But I don't see—"

"I want to open a camp," he said bluntly. "For foster kids. Boys specifically, though I'm not opposed to girls. Just don't know how good I'd be around a bunch of girls. But that's why I bought the house, the property, and why I'm renovating and…well, I'd like to give them some part of what Russ and Elaine gave me." He pulled in a breath. "And I guess that's it."

Another full-on blast of emotion enveloped Haley. "You're an amazing man, Gavin Daugherty. Absolutely freaking amazing. And you don't even know, don't even realize."

This time, she couldn't stop the tears that filled her eyes. Didn't much care to, though. Because for a man with Gavin's past to want to take those experiences and turn them into something so positive, so affirming, was…well, as she'd said: amazing.

Wondrous, too.

"Don't see where you get amazing from that," he said, sounding embarrassed. "Just feels important. Like what I'm supposed to do, so that's what I'm doing."

"It is important. And…thank you for sharing this. For wanting to share this." Then, she gathered her strength, her courage, and said, "Can I ask another question? One that sort of goes along with the 'you're too busy for distractions' thing?"

"Can't we talk about something easy? Like…why the world didn't end on December 21, 2012? Or the 'Which came first, the chicken or the egg?' dilemma? Or we could ask each other thought-provoking questions, such as, 'If you could have any superpower, which would it be?'"

Okay. Obviously, she'd pushed too hard for one night.

"Sure," she said easily. "I'm partial to the superpower question. But it's sort of hard to choose, with so many possible—"

"That night, when I went to the bar asking for you," Gavin interrupted, rushing through the words, as if he feared he wouldn't say them otherwise, "Dylan told your father that you were out on a date. The news didn't sit so well with me."

Oh. Darn Dylan. He couldn't have just said that she wasn't home?

"This…helps me understand some. But, Gavin, this is so easily explained." Haley then went on to describe the details of the weirder-than-weird blind date, ending with, "I really didn't want to go. I would've much rather been with you."

Shifting, he wrapped his arm around her shoulders, brought her closer, so her head now rested on his chest. "That's sweet of you, and I appreciate the explanation. Once I thought about it some, I figured you wouldn't have kissed me if you were interested in someone else. But my reaction to hearing about the date…well, that stayed with me."

She thought about how she would feel if she learned Gavin was out on a date, the night after their first kiss, and a strong, instant gush of jealousy smacked her upside the head. No. She wouldn't have liked that one bit, but unlike Gavin, she would've said something to him.

The first chance she'd had, even. But, as she'd just heard, their lives were incredibly different, and while she didn't—couldn't—fully put herself in his shoes, she thought she understood what had happened. Maybe, what was still happening.

His mother had let him down repeatedly, horrifically. He'd grown up mostly in homes that weren't really homes, excepting for Russ and Elaine's. Just…places to sleep, she guessed. She thought about what Suzette had said, about her fear of Matt hurting her, and pieces of the puzzle began to fit together, began to paint a picture.

It was time, Haley decided, to put her cards on the table. Faceup. So Gavin knew, without a doubt, where she stood. Whether he'd believe her or not was another question.

"I understand, I think," she said, working out the words as she went along. "And I don't know where you're at, and I don't know what you think of me. Feel for me. But I'm serious about this, about you, and…you should know I've never felt so strongly about a man before."

She waited, tense and afraid, for his response. Minutes ticked by without a word, and each second increased her fear. But he didn't stop holding her, didn't push her away, so she tried to believe those were positive signs, tried to keep her breathing calm, and just waited.

Finally, when she was sure she should've kept her mouth shut for a little longer, he said, "I think of you well. And often. You're… Hell, Haley, you're in my head more than you're not. But we're different, and that worries me some, wondering how that could possibly work."

"We are different. Very different."

"And there are times you completely rattle me."

"Trust me," she said, still tense. Still afraid of where this might lead. "You know how to rattle a person, too. So, I suppose we have that in common."

A soft laugh emerged. "I suppose we do. And see…I know how this sounds, hate saying this to you, but I don't necessarily believe you have these feelings."

"Oh. So you think I'm lying?"

"No. Not that. I… Dammit." His arm tightened around her. "Other than Russ and Elaine, I don't have a lot of experience with folks…with people caring. I don't think you're lying. I wonder, I guess, if what you think you see, feel, is the truth. Or if you're—"

"Deluding myself? Um, no." Now she pulled out of his grasp, turned to face him. Wished it was light enough that he could see her eyes, where she was sure the strength of her emotions, her surety, would be visible. "I know what makes up a good man. And Gavin, you're one of the best men I've ever met. Hands down. I also know myself, very well. So, if you're not quite able to see what I see, then try to trust that I'm being honest. Wholly honest."

"I don't want to hurt you," he admitted gruffly. "Don't want to let you down."

She thought about that some, too, decided to be even blunter. "Do you care about me?"

"Yes. I care…a hell of a lot more than what makes sense."

"Then why not try? Why can't we take this one day at a time and see where we end up?" She breathed in, counted to three. "I'm not asking for guarantees. Not asking you to do anything other than try. And… Well, to talk to me. Rather than sending another idiotic email."

"Try, huh? That's all you want from me, nothing else?"

"For now, yes. For a long while, yes. And if you're trying, if *we're* trying, then I don't see how you can let me down. Or, for that matter, how I can let you down." Leaning close to him, she laid her hand on his cheek. "This is a two-way street. I'd like to see where it leads."

"I wouldn't mind knowing that myself."

"So," she said, her heart beating fast, hard, "do we have another deal?"

"I… Yes. We do."

Suddenly, his arms were around her and he was kissing her. Again with intensity, with passion, with all of the emotion that had just made up their conversation. Her body eased against his, and somehow, without her quite knowing how, she was in his lap with her legs wrapped around him, without their mouths separating from each other for more than a second.

Love. It was here, between them, vibrant and alive and

potent, growing in strength as they kissed, until the weight of the emotion was solid and real and miraculous.

Everlasting, too, she hoped.

Gavin groaned, pulled back some, and said, "I don't have… That is, I was expecting a weekend with Suzette Solomon, not you, so I didn't bring—"

"Protection?" Haley said, breathless and tingling. "I did. In various colors, even."

There was that warm, rich laugh. "Of course you did."

He kissed her again, long and tantalizing and filled with promises, before leading her to the tent, where they spent another sleepless night. This time, though, in each other's arms.

Chapter Twelve

Rubbing his hand over his newly shaven jaw, Gavin stared at the envelope his mother had left with him. A lot of changes were happening fast, almost one right on top of the other, and so far, he thought he'd handled a good chunk of them fairly well.

Not without concern or some anxiety. Not without that god-awful feeling of free-falling without a safety net, but all in all, better than he'd have expected of himself. Due to Haley, really, and her unrelenting positivity. She just seemed so sure of him, of them, that he kept pushing a slew of his reservations aside in favor of…tenuous hope.

In the almost two weeks since she'd finagled her way into sharing a single tent with him, they had spent some portion of most days together…and a few of the nights. Those nights were beyond description, or, at least, beyond anything Gavin had known before. Sex with Haley was physically pleasurable, no doubt, but also…satiated him on a deeper level.

He didn't know how to express what that meant, exactly, but he recognized the importance. Recognized the rarity of such a connection. And hell, even that scared him.

When they weren't in bed, they were usually talking about one thing or the other. Lately, she'd been real interested in his plans for the camp, had offered to help—with research, with his renovations. With his business, too. And while he knew she meant the offers and would likely bend herself into a pretzel making good on them, he always declined.

Agreeing, letting her more fully in, would require a lot of faith. He'd have to completely push past his defenses, and he couldn't quite force himself to go there. Sometimes, he didn't think he'd ever get to the point where that would feel doable. Though, when he was with Haley—awash in her energy and belief—trying came easier. Seemed less impossible than those moments he was stuck in his own head, running through the possible outcomes.

Those worst-case scenarios that refused to dissipate.

Part of that, he knew, had to do with the fact that his mother was in Steamboat Springs. How could he focus on the present, on a possible future with a woman, with her so close by? Waiting for him to make a decision he wasn't sure he had it in him to make.

Or, he supposed, a decision he might not want to make. He'd told Haley the truth: the past was the past, and he didn't see a lot of sense in sifting through the dirt.

But the thought of his mother sitting in an apartment, in a city that wasn't her own, waiting for him to show up at her door, was beginning to weigh hard and heavy. He picked up the envelope and turned it over, to the flap side, and almost... almost gave in and opened the darn thing. The second he started picking at the sealed flap, an invisible fist slammed into his gut and all of those old feelings resurfaced, damn near choking him with their strength, their negativity.

Nope. He couldn't do it. Couldn't force himself to willingly walk into that world of misery again. Couldn't bear to confront the demons he'd shoved into the closet.

Especially now. *Specifically* now.

So he didn't. He tossed the envelope back on top of his dresser and stalked from his bedroom, ignoring the deluge of guilt that the decision brought on. He had absolutely nothing to feel guilty about. Not one blasted thing. His mother was here of her own accord. She had kept him waiting for years, had given him false hope time after time.

She could wait on him now, while he sorted through the garbage and figured out what—if anything at all—he was capable of.

Stretching her neck from side to side, Haley only half listened as her brother Cole finished breaking down the past month's numbers for the sporting goods store. They always had their family meetings at the restaurant, after closing, and typically shared a late meal. This particular meeting had extended later than normal, as they'd had to skip the last one due to incompatible schedules and the crazy summer working hours.

Everyone was here: her parents, Cole and his fiancée, Rachel, Reid and Dylan. They'd eaten first and had kept their conversation social, as these dinners also served as family time. Once dessert was served, though, her dad had started the business portion of the night, and one by one, each person had the opportunity to express concerns and ideas, and give updates.

Tonight, she was having considerable difficulty staying focused. Her thoughts were, naturally, mostly consumed by Gavin, their weekend camping trip and each day since. On the surface, their relationship seemed to be progressing well.

There were shared meals, conversations, walks on his property and some—frankly speaking—amazing sex.

Really amazing sex. Bone-deep satisfying sex that was at once deliciously, physically pleasurable with the heat and energy their bodies created when together, and the intensely emotional completeness that existed only when two souls belonged together.

So yes, the good was quite good. Better than good.

But she had this strange, niggling worry that everything wasn't as solid as it seemed, and that while Gavin was trying, he was also…holding back, still determined to keep her at a distance. She'd analyzed about every minute they'd spent together, and couldn't quite put her finger on why she had this worry. Yet the feeling persisted and, in fact, continued to grow.

"Haley? Are you in there somewhere?" her father asked, breaking into her thoughts. "Is there anything on your agenda to discuss tonight?"

"Um. What? Sorry, I was thinking about…" Her brain faltered, searching for what she'd planned on broaching at tonight's meeting. Oh. "I've decided, if everyone is on board, I'd like to pass over a larger portion of the accounting responsibilities to Rebecca," she said, naming her cousin Seth's wife. "Seems silly not to. We have a CPA in the family, and she'll be more expedient, accurate, than I am."

There was some discussion on this, along with a few questions, but in the end—as Haley had fully expected—the decision was agreed to and set. All that remained was arranging a phone meeting with Rebecca, since she lived in Washington State, to hash out the remaining details.

But when Haley mentioned that her salary should be lowered, no one agreed. After all, as her father explained, she was an equal partner and she worked far more hours during the summer and winter seasons in roles that weren't specifically her responsibilities. Since this was an accurate assessment, Haley stopped arguing and the discussion ended.

She assumed they were nearing the end of the meeting, so she leaned back in her chair and breathed a sigh of relief. Really, she just wanted to run upstairs and call Gavin. Find out how the rest of his day had gone, and—hopefully—make plans for tomorrow.

Except, rather than ending the meeting, her father once again focused on her. "One more thing, Haley. I wanted to ask you about that Gavin fellow. Everything working out fairly well?

A whole bunch of curious eyes landed on her. She coughed. Twirled her hair with her finger. "Um." What, exactly, was her father asking? "Yes. I think so. Why do you ask?"

"Gavin who?" Reid asked. "And is what working out well?"

"Daugherty, I believe he said his last name was," her father supplied. "Came in here a while back, looking for Haley. Mentioned he'd—"

"Gavin Daugherty?" Cole's gaze narrowed in speculation. In the way that told Haley he'd recognized the name, was searching his memory for where he knew it from.

Haley slid down in her chair a tad. He'd remember in one… two…three—"

"Got it! Gavin's the guy who came into the store last winter. The one you just about begged me to hire, even though we didn't need another instructor. That's him, right?" Cole said, his tone suggesting he already knew the answer. "The very same guy you got all goofy over, stormed into the back and slammed the door. If, that is, I'm recalling correctly."

"Goofy? I believe your recollection is off by a mile. Or more," she said as flippantly as possible. "But yes, that was Gavin. And I still think you should've hired him."

"Didn't have the need," Cole pointed out. "Maybe this next winter, if he's still looking."

"He won't be. He's all set now. Works at the hardware store, and has his own business. Guiding folks on hikes, white-water rafting trips...camping." Her cheeks warmed as she spoke, as the image of camping with Gavin resurfaced. "In the winter, he'll offer ski instruction and...and—" She stopped, drew in a breath. "You should've hired him when you could."

"It's him," Dylan said, entering the fray. "This is the guy you've been mooning over."

"Wait a minute here." Reid shook his head in confusion. "I'm lost. Someone explain."

Paul Foster settled his hands on the table, fingers laced together. "Gavin came in here looking for Haley. He mentioned something about promotional ideas, so I assumed he'd hired her for some design work. Now," he said, directing his gaze at Haley, "I'm rather confused, myself. Are you two personally involved, sweetheart?"

Squeezing her eyes shut, Haley silently counted to three. She'd planned on introducing her family to Gavin, but she'd wanted to wait until summer ended. When everyone's lives calmed down. When her relationship with Gavin had grown some.

But here it was, so why put off the inevitable?

She opened her eyes, nodded. "Yes. We're involved. We've been...dating."

Everyone began talking at once, asking questions and offering opinions. She kept her mouth shut and waited for a natural lull. She had more to say, more she planned on saying, but any attempts at being heard over the roar of noise would just prove futile.

When the lull came to be, she lifted her chin. "Gavin is important to me, which is why I haven't said anything about him before. I love you all, but you can be a bit overwhelming at times. Especially for someone who isn't accustomed to—" she gestured her hand around the table "—all of this. And he isn't. He's…sort of a loner."

Uh-oh. Wrong word to use, even if the description was accurate.

More questions, more comments, more concerns expressed. So she answered the questions the best she could. Initially, they weren't difficult to answer. Dylan wanted to know more about how they'd met. Her mother wanted to know when they'd started dating. Cole asked some questions about Gavin's business. But when her father, and then Reid, started asking about Gavin's family, his past—where he'd lived before moving to Steamboat Springs, his reasons for moving here…she couldn't, wouldn't, supply the answers. Not even those she knew.

Sharing any piece of what Gavin had told her about his mother, growing up in various foster homes, and his dreams for the camp he hoped to start, seemed wrong. This information was private and had been difficult enough for him to tell her, and she knew he'd barely brushed the surface. So, no. She was not going to answer these questions.

Instead, feeling somewhat desperate, she changed the direction of the conversation with, "Actually, back to Cole's question. I really think we should consider developing a collaboration with Gavin's business. A partnership of sorts, where we refer spillover customers to each other, share in the profits…maybe help him out with equipment needs."

"You're trying to avoid answering my questions," Reid said. "Dad's, too. What is there about this guy that you don't want us to know?"

"Nothing. But my relationship with him is private, and any further details—details he should talk about, not me—are not up for discussion." She pushed out an exasperated sigh. "Besides which, it's getting late and I'd like to go to bed sometime soon."

Reid was all set to argue, she could plainly see the fact of that in his expression, in the hard way in which he held his jaw. Fortunately, their mother must have decided enough was enough. With a brisk smack on the table, all eyes turned to her.

"Haley is right," Margaret said. "While I would love to know more about the man my daughter is dating, there is plenty of time for that." Pausing, she looked in Haley's direction. "We'll have him over for dinner. Soon. We can meet him, discuss these other ideas of yours more fully and have a pleasant evening. You'll let me know which night works best for him?"

Her tone bore no room for argument. Not even wiggling room.

"Of course," Haley responded, her stomach sinking. "I'm sure he'll be...pleased."

"Good," her mother said, smiling brightly. "I can't wait to meet him."

Rachel winked at Haley from across the table and offered her a small, comforting smile. She'd always adored Rachel, long before she had become her brother's fiancée. Cole and Rachel had been friends for almost forever, so Haley had already considered her a sister when their relationship became romantic. Even if she was blonde and beautiful, and had a designer wardrobe that, in the past, had sent Haley into...well, rather girlish fits of delight.

"Cole and I have some news we'd like to share," Rachel was saying. She squeezed Cole's arm, and a light blush spread along her cheeks. "Rather exciting news."

"That's right, we do!" Cole wrapped his arm over Rachel's shoulder, and cleared his throat authoritatively. "Rach and I have—drumroll, please—set our wedding date. We've decided on spring. April nineteenth, to be exact, so everyone mark your calendars."

And then, the bedlam started again. A happier, less tense bedlam than when all the intensity of the Fosters had been focused on Haley, on her relationship with Gavin.

Well, except for Reid. He continued to watch her steadily, with questions and concern in his eyes, coating his expression. She pretended she didn't notice, pretended to be involved in discussing Cole and Rachel's wedding plans, pretended to not have a care in the world.

In truth, she couldn't stop thinking—worrying—about Gavin's reaction when she told him she'd brought up the partnership idea without getting his go-ahead first. Still, even if her family ended up agreeing, Gavin could always say no. That wasn't the issue.

Heck, he didn't even want her help in painting walls, or building a new website for his business, or in planning, researching for the camp he wanted to start. So this, she knew, would not go over well. On the other hand, he'd flat-out told her he didn't want her to change for anyone, so maybe… maybe she was stressing too much. Maybe this would be okay, too.

Then, assuming they moved past that not-so-little dilemma, there was the matter of preparing him for dinner with her family. Meeting the whole crew of them at once hadn't been Haley's plan. She'd hoped to introduce him to her parents when the time came, then maybe Rachel and Cole, and then later to Reid and Dylan. Ease Gavin into the family one person at a time, not throw him in headfirst.

Haley forcibly shoved her concerns aside. For one, there was nothing she could do about any of it now. For another, she trusted Gavin and she trusted her family. She didn't have any doubts that, given time, her parents and brothers would recognize all of Gavin's amazing qualities, or that Gavin would see the same qualities in each member of her family.

Right. That would happen.

As long as Gavin didn't decree the road too bumpy and filled with potholes to bother traveling. As long as he didn't decide to step off and take a different, less complicated path.

One that didn't include Haley.

Late Saturday morning found Gavin walking the aisles at the hardware store, tidying up shelves and helping customers as needed. His shift ended in a few hours, and then he was meeting Haley for coffee at the Beanery. He missed her. They hadn't seen each other over the past several days, as she'd been up to her neck working crazy hours.

Whenever they'd talked, though, she hadn't been her normal, exuberant self. A fact that had raised his concern a good several levels. As much as he tried to ignore the negative thoughts, he couldn't stop wondering if she was finally having those doubts he felt sure she'd eventually have. Doubts about him, them, if she'd made a mistake that first day when she'd followed him home. And every day, every action she'd taken, since then.

He could be wrong. She could be tired, nothing more.

But all these worries did was maximize his discomfort in allowing her more into his life than he already had. He wanted to let her in. All the way in, if truth be told. It was difficult, though, wanting something—someone—so much, when he feared what would happen if she changed her mind and walked away. He knew that particular type of pain too damn well.

Today would help. Spending some one-on-one time with Haley would ease his concerns, would help him set aside that strangling sense of the inevitable. Seeing her always gave him an electric jolt of positivity that muffled his fears over what could go wrong.

Noticing that a customer had, in his attempts to find whatever they were looking for, left a display of various tool sets askew, he began reorganizing the boxes, lost in thought. Had just finished when he heard someone approach, stop behind him.

"Excuse me," the man said, "are you Gavin Daugherty?"

Turning, Gavin nodded. Only took a second to recognize the owner of the voice. "That would be me," he said evenly, surprised by the visit. Curious, too.

"Reid Foster," the man said. "Haley's brother?"

"Yup. I recognized you right off." He reached out, shook Reid's hand. "Haley speaks real highly of you. Cole and Dylan, as well. So…what can I do for you?"

"Well, I was wondering if you had a break coming up, or some time later, maybe tomorrow or the next day, to sit down and talk. I don't want to keep you from work," Reid said, his tone also even. Friendly enough, though.

Gavin looked around, noted the store wasn't overly busy. "I have a few minutes now."

"Here? Or…is there somewhere we can have a little privacy?"

"Here's fine. Say what you need to say."

This, Gavin's willingness to discuss whatever the man wanted to discuss in a public venue, seemed to give Reid pause. He ran his hand over his jaw, gave Gavin an assessing type of look, before saying, "If you're sure."

"I'm sure."

"Okay, then," he said. "Well, see, it's like this. Haley doesn't tend to be secretive about much of anything. My sister has a thought in her head, and she shares it with anyone who will listen. But with you, she's been secretive. That causes me some worry."

"I imagine that's normal," Gavin said, trying to put himself in Reid's shoes. Thinking maybe this impromptu visit was nothing more than a way for Reid to satisfy his curiosity, and therefore some of his worry. "She's your sister, and you don't know me."

"This is true. And…look, this is an uncomfortable situation, and I dislike behaving in this manner. But she's my sister, and…" Reid glanced around, as if to ascertain they were still basically alone. They were. "My concern pushed me into doing a little digging."

"And you did this how?" Not that Gavin particularly cared, but it gave him something to say while he processed what Reid might have discovered, what he might be leading to.

"One of those online information-gathering sources. The type that gives you addresses, employment history and the like. And I discovered you've moved around a lot, which isn't abnormal for a guy who makes his living on the slopes during the winter, the mountains and rivers in the summer. That…well, that didn't bother me at all. Something else did."

A muscle in Gavin's jaw began to tick. Now he knew exactly where this conversation was headed. The path he'd nearly taken when Gavin had received the letter from Russ's estate. "You're talking about Aspen," he said matter-of-factly. "And that I worked for a company where a whole mess of illegal practices were taking place."

"That is exactly what I'm referring to." Reid narrowed his eyes. "Don't know if you know this, but I'm a ski patroller. Meaning, my job is all about safety. So when I hear about a company renting substandard equipment to unsuspecting customers, hiring folks without the proper training or skill to keep those same customers safe…well, I get a little worked up."

"Don't blame you for that. Bothers me, too."

"Were you a part of the misconduct? Aware of it?"

"Not a part of it, no. Unaware of it for most of the season, yes. Toward the end, I realized what was going on." Meeting the other man's eyes head-on, Gavin said, "And I did not react as quickly as I should have."

He'd been angrier than all get-out when he'd discovered the truth, and was all set to go to the authorities. But the owner of the company offered him money to keep his mouth shut, to leave Aspen and not look back. Gavin was ashamed to admit he'd considered the offer, for longer than he should have. A good couple of days or so.

People could've been hurt in those couple of days. They weren't, thank God, but they could've been. And if so, that responsibility would've rested on Gavin's shoulders. Fortunately, Russ's letter had arrived, and those words...the belief Russ had in him, woke him the hell up.

And he did what was right.

"I see," Reid said. "But you did react?"

"I did. Went to the authorities, gave them the information." The place was shut down quickly enough. Temporarily at first, while the investigation was going on, and then for good.

"Well, I suppose that's something." Another long, rather intense appraisal before Reid said, "Feel like explaining why you waited? What happened to push you forward when you did?"

"Not so much, no." Gavin didn't elaborate. If Haley asked...he'd try to open up with her, try to tell her everything, but he felt no need to explain himself to her older brother. "You wanted to know if I was a willing participant in something illegal. I wasn't. That should be enough."

"I suppose it should be."

"Will have to be," Gavin said, his voice steady. Inside, he was a jumble of contradictions. Again. Haley's family was important to her, as they should be. If Reid didn't approve of Gavin, it might make Haley rethink everything. "I should get back to work now, though."

"Understood. Appreciate the time."

Gavin watched Reid make his way toward the front of the store, sure as he could be that this conversation would be repeated to Haley verbatim sometime soon. Possibly raising all of those doubts he kept waiting for her to have.

Well, then, he'd just prepare himself for that scenario. If he could.

Chapter Thirteen

Wow. Just wow. Haley sat across from Gavin at the Beanery and stared, unable to take in the changes to his appearance. She'd thought him handsome with the beard, with the almost-but-not-quite-long hair, but she had to admit his clean-shaven, strong-angled-jaw, shorter-hair look raised that assessment several notches. He was drop-dead gorgeous.

They'd met out front about thirty minutes ago, and after her fairly vocal response to his new look, they'd gotten their coffees. Since then, she'd tried to stop staring and focus on the conversation, on identifying the strange energy she felt emanating from Gavin. So far, no luck in those areas. She was also working toward the discussion they needed to have, about her family, the dinner and how she'd broached the idea of a partnership with them.

None of which she particularly wanted to talk about. At least, not until she understood the tension, distance, hovering between them. She hated the distance most of all.

"Everything okay with you today?" she asked for the third time. "You seem quiet."

"Yup. Just feeling quiet, I guess." He swallowed a long gulp of his coffee. Then, apparently deciding to divert her attention, he said, "I've been meaning to ask you about your favorite Christmas memory. Keep forgetting, but I'd like to know."

"Sure." She'd play along. Perhaps, once they'd chatted for a while, the mood would lighten and she'd find her feet. "I'd have to say my favorite Christmas memory is the Christmas Eve I was ten. I'd been sick all day with a cold, my parents had been gone most of the day at the restaurant. Reid was there, took care of me, kept me occupied the best he could."

"Sounds as if Reid was more like another parent to you," Gavin said, an odd note to his voice she couldn't name. "Rather than just an older brother."

"Oh, he was. Is. But on this day, I was miserable, and I didn't want him. I wanted my mother. And oh, did I whine." Haley laughed, thinking back. "Sick kids tend to want their mothers, as I'm sure you remember—" *Crap.* "I'm so sorry. So sorry I said that."

"It's okay, Haley." She didn't believe him. Not with the stilted, stiff way he spoke. Not with the shield that had just slammed over his expression. "Go on. Tell me about the memory."

"Um, right. Well, Reid let me fall asleep on the couch that evening, so I could see my parents as soon as they walked in." Now, she just wanted to get the rest of the telling out as quickly as possible. Wanted to mitigate whatever hurt she'd caused. "And when I opened my eyes, they were standing there, and my father was holding mistletoe over my mom's head, and they were kissing. I just remember feeling so secure, so…happy they were home."

He nodded but didn't speak. His skin paled a shade. Her

heart ached with sadness, again for the boy he'd once been. Again, for the man that boy had become.

Dammit. Why hadn't she thought this memory through before sharing it? Gavin's life hadn't involved loving parents kissing under the mistletoe. She should've made something up, or just told a lame story about receiving a much-wanted gift. Something else. Anything other than a piece of her happy family history.

She reached over, grasped his hand with hers. What she wouldn't give to go back in time and alter his past. Give him a new childhood. One filled to the brim with happy memories.

"Don't look so sad, Haley," Gavin said, his voice a rumble of emotion. "It's good you have such a great family. I'm glad for that, for you. Really. Would be wrong if you couldn't talk about your family or your memories with me."

Even so, the weight of her sadness didn't ease. She just felt bad. In as bright a voice as she could pull off, she said, "Well, now you know my favorite Christmas memory."

"That I do." As he had in front of the campfire, he rubbed the palm of her hand with his thumb, the warmth of his touch returning some of her balance. "I… Your brother came by the hardware store today. Surprised me. Seems barging in on folks is part of the Foster DNA," he said with a small laugh. "He…well, I thought you should know, since he'll proba-bly—"

"Which brother?" she interjected.

"Reid."

Of course. She should've known. "What did he want?"

Not that it mattered. Not really. But this annoyed her. Hugely. And Reid was going to get a strong piece of her mind the next time she saw him. Maybe a kick in the rear, too.

"He asked a few questions about my past. Had some con-cerns he wanted to discuss."

"Let me guess," she said, her aggravation increasing by

the second. How dare Reid take it upon himself to approach Gavin? Now the odd energy made sense. As did the distance. "He told you about the family dinner, which I haven't even had a chance to talk to you about yet. And he likely wanted to know more about your past because of the partnership possibility, and—"

"Wait," Gavin said abruptly, with a definite edge to his tone. "What did you just say?"

Double crap. No. Make that *triple* crap. "Um, so that isn't why Reid came to see you?"

"If so, he didn't utter a word of any of it." Dropping her hand, Gavin tapped his fingers against the tabletop in agitation. "I told you I'm not interested in a partnership. Why would you start the ball rolling with your family if you knew this? I don't—" He swore softly. "You should have, if nothing else, talked with me first. I should have met everyone first."

"You're right. I didn't plan on broaching any of it, not at all."

"Then why did you?"

"Well, I hadn't really talked about us. And…basically, it came out that we're involved." Inhaling a breath, Haley tried to calm down, to stop talking so fast. "Reid and my father started asking questions about where you lived before moving here, why you moved here, your family, and I didn't want to answer those questions. It didn't seem right or fair and—"

A slight woman with medium brown hair caught Haley's attention. She hovered to the side of their table, just out of Gavin's line of vision, but she stared at him with such intensity, such yearning, that Haley lost her train of thought. Her intuition kicked in, hard, and she reached for Gavin's hand, wanting to warn him of…something she, again, couldn't name.

The woman gave her head a small shake, turned on her

heel—as if to leave—and then stopped, turned around again. And approached the table.

"Gavin," Haley whispered, clutching his hand. "There's—"

"I wasn't going to say hi, but you're here...and I have an interview in a few minutes," Vanessa said, stopping next to the table. "So. I'm saying hi. I hope that's okay."

Gavin's heart thudded in that too-fast, too-hard beat. He couldn't seem to breathe for a second. An interview? Certainly that couldn't mean what first came to mind. She probably just needed some extra cash in order to stick around for so long.

Didn't mean she was staying...couldn't mean that.

And this, seeing her now without any sort of notice, turned up the volume of his discomfort. His mother hadn't stopped by the house again, hadn't phoned. So he supposed he couldn't blame her for running into him in a public place, but he did. The last thing he needed now was to add her—her hopes, that desperate need written all over her—into the mix.

"I'm in the middle of something right now," he said with as little emotion as possible. Not that easy. Not with the conversation he'd had with Reid, or the unpleasant aftertaste the encounter had left him with. Definitely not with the conversation he was currently having with Haley, or with the downward spiral of his thoughts. "So, if you'll excuse us."

Haley darted him a question-filled glance. She leaned across the table, toward his mother, and held out her hand. "I'm Haley," she said in her typical cheerful manner. Well, not wholly cheerful. He heard the underlying twinge of concern clear enough. "Did you say you have an interview here? I always thought this would be a great place to work. Lola's fantastic."

"I'm Vanessa." She appeared unsure, ill-at-ease, but she shook Haley's hand. "Vanessa Daugherty, Gavin's...mother. And yes, I have an interview with Lola."

"Y-you're Gavin's mother?" Blinking, she looked at Gavin. "This is your *mother?*"

"Yes," Gavin said, offering no additional details.

"I am," Vanessa replied.

"This is a…surprise. I hadn't realized you were in town." Another series of blinks before Haley sat up a little straighter. "How long are you visiting for?"

"That depends." With an air of defiance, Vanessa focused her attention on him. He resisted the urge to squirm or look away. "I'm hoping to find a job, Gavin. Assuming I do, I've decided to stay in Steamboat Springs permanently. I like the area, and it seems a good place for a fresh start. And…I like knowing I'm close to you. Mileage-wise, if nothing else."

Shock hit him first, causing the room's walls to seemingly close in on him, and he had to fight real hard to stay centered, to keep his disquiet tamped down. A solid dose of nausea kicked in next. All at the news that his mother might stay in Steamboat Springs.

How in the hell was he supposed to react to such a possibility? Or, for that matter, to Haley's all-too-visible surprise and disappointment? In him, he knew. She was disappointed in *him,* and he couldn't blame her. Not one bit. Probably he should've mentioned his mother's visit. Should've tried to talk about this with Haley. Warned her, at least.

"I suppose if that's what you want," he said to his mother, "then that's what you should do. Doesn't change my end of this."

"I'm aware, and I want a lot more than that," she said quietly, firmly. "But what I want and what I have the right to expect are two different things, aren't they?"

Well, at least they were in accord on that subject. Didn't help in this moment, though. Didn't give him even a second of peace. "Good luck, then. With the interview."

Why'd he go and wish her luck? He couldn't care less if

she stayed in Steamboat Springs. Could he? No, of course not. The thought was absurd.

"Thank you," she said, her voice holding that almost-but-not-quite-breaking quality that always tore into him, always made him wish—again—that their relationship wasn't what it was. "I...hope to see you soon. Please think about it."

"I have been. Will keep thinking on it, too. Can't make you any other promises."

She opened her mouth as if she were going to say something else, but didn't. Just nodded in farewell and walked away from the table. Unfortunately, the damage was done. Unfortunately, he felt zero relief. He couldn't think, couldn't process all that had happened today. Especially couldn't come to terms with the prospect of his mother remaining in the city he'd chosen as his sanctuary, *his* fresh start. Wasn't supposed to be hers.

"Why... That is, how long has your mother been in town?" Haley asked.

"Weeks," he said shortly. "She's been here for weeks."

"Weeks? You haven't said anything. Not even one word." Disbelief and hurt colored her words. "I didn't even know you were still in contact with her. What does she want?"

"She's sober now. Has been for several years, and she wants to make amends," he said, battling with his frustration at trying to explain something he didn't know how to explain. "I haven't yet decided if I'm interested, which is why I haven't mentioned any of this to you."

Haley closed her eyes for a millisecond. She breathed in, and then out. "Can we talk about this? How do you feel at the possibility of your mother living here?"

Sinking as he was, Gavin took a moment to level out some, to think about what he wanted to do here. Truth was, he wanted to confide in Haley. Taking that step, though, felt threatening. Dangerous. Risky and illogical, based on the sum knowledge of his experiences. She wouldn't understand, couldn't even come close to understanding. How could she?

Their lives bore zero similarities. She had a close, loving family who had her back. A lifetime of experiences that were, unlike Gavin's, mostly positive. How could any of this work? How could a relationship between two people with such different views on themselves, on the world itself, have even the slightest shot at being successful? He just didn't see how.

"I don't want to talk about this, Haley," he said, suddenly exhausted. With everything. This conversation, Haley's belief, his mother's hope. Everything. "You won't understand."

Temper—good and hot—bled into her eyes, in the tilt of her chin. "You could give me a chance before making such a statement. No, Gavin, I can't understand some of this—maybe not a lot of this—the way you can. But I can listen, and support you, and offer an opinion from a different perspective. Those are valuable, as well. And dammit, I just wish you'd try."

"I have been trying." Hell, that was all he seemed to do. *Try*. And really, where had that gotten him? All of this trying had stripped away the tools he used to manage, to remain steady and focused and…in control. Frustration piled inside, merging with the rest of the mess he had brewing. "You ignore half the stuff I tell you, anyway. The flyers, the camping trip, the partnership idea. I'm not altogether sure that you *do* listen."

"Unfair," she said in a near sob. And that sob, the fact he had her so close to crying, split his heart into two. Made him feel like a heel. Again brought up all of those realities he kept trying to avoid. "We've already discussed the flyers and the camping trip, so unfair to toss those in. You have a point with the other, though, and I wasn't done explaining. Let me explain."

"No need to," he said. "I heard enough. I understand

enough of what happened. And I know your heart is in the right place, but I believe I've told you before that I prefer to be prepared."

"Right," she said. "You have, and I *did* listen. I just… I thought—" She breathed in, looked down at the table. "You're right. I've pushed and pried my way into your life and I've ignored many of your wishes. I'm sorry. I shouldn't have taken it upon myself to do most of what I've done, even if my… heart was in the right place."

"I wasn't angling for an apology," he said gruffly.

"Okay, but my apology is sincere."

He knew what he needed to do. This woman was important to him, and here she was almost crying because of his inability to give her what she needed, what she deserved. Wasn't her fault he was who he was. Wasn't her fault he couldn't be the person she saw him as.

Nope. None of this was her fault.

And if they kept on, he'd end up hurting her again and again, because he couldn't be the man she deserved. Couldn't be the type of man her family would want her to be with. Hell, he couldn't be the type of man *he* thought she should be with. And that…that left one option.

Only one.

The decision settled some of his whipped-up emotions, even if that same decision burned in his chest like a soldering iron. He breathed air deep into his lungs to cool the burn, to settle himself more. Relaxed his muscles one by one until he believed he'd be able to speak with assurance.

"This isn't working, Haley. We aren't working," he said, speaking as clear and absolute as he knew how. "You're a remarkable, beautiful woman, but…I'm not the man for you. So I see zero sense in pretending otherwise. But I tried. I really did. I guess…well, I guess I'm just not built for this. But you should know—need to know—that I wish I was."

Shock rippled through her body. "You are not doing this to me again."

"I'm sorry, Haley. I really am." And because he couldn't think through his pain, couldn't find any other explanation than what he'd already said, he repeated, "I'm not the man for you."

"You're wrong. You are the man for me. And you are built for this. You just can't see it yet." Her tears fell then, cascading down her cheeks in a rush. A soft gurgle of pain, disbelief, fell from her throat. "Don't do this, Gavin."

"I have to. It's the right choice." Swallowing, he forced himself to remain calm. Absolute. If he showed her even a hint of his turmoil, misery, then she'd find a way to convince him to keep going. To keep trying. And he couldn't—wouldn't— do that to her. To him, either.

Not when they'd just end up here anyway. As he'd learned from his mother, false hope did no one a bit of good. False hope brought on more pain each and every time that hope was destroyed. Until eventually, all that remained was the hollow, empty, lonely place he lived in.

Nope. Haley would not live in the same place. He wouldn't allow it.

"This is the right choice," he said again. "I need you to accept this."

"You're so wrong." Tears still slid and slipped down the planes of her face. She wiped them away, sucked in a shaky breath and gave him that stubborn-as-hell look he so loved. "I won't ignore your wishes this time, and I won't chase after you again. This is a cycle I won't keep repeating."

"Good," he said, doing his best to ignore the riptide of pain that was about three seconds from swallowing him whole. "You shouldn't."

"What I will do is hope you change your mind," she said,

her chin high. "And I will hope you find the sense to do so soon. But you'll have to come to me."

And then, without a backward glance, she stood and walked away.

When Haley walked into the back door at Foster's Pub and Grill, the first person her eyes landed on was Reid. Just seeing him, standing there talking to one of the employees as if her world hadn't just exploded around her, brought every one of her emotions to the edge. And no, this wasn't his fault. Not really. But she couldn't see the logic.

Not with her agony, her despair, her surety that she had just lost someone so essential, so crucial to her happiness, to who she was, that she'd never smile again.

So she wasn't thinking when she approached him. She wasn't considering all of the other reasons—whether valid or invalid—why Gavin had just made this decision. All she saw, all she felt, was that she had to blame *someone*. And Reid was the likeliest candidate.

"How dare you?" she all but yelled. "What gives you the right to butt your head into my life without even so much as talking with me? Do you know what you've done?"

"Whoa there, Haley," Reid said, instantly concerned. Instantly defensive, too. "I don't know what you think I did, but other than a few questions—"

"Oh, no, you don't get to 'whoa' me. Not this time." Haley's breaths became ragged as her brain formed the words she needed to say. "This man is amazing, Reid. You don't even know. Don't even have the slightest clue what you've done... or, at least, the part you've played in what has just happened. I...I've had to work so hard to...to just get him to give me—us—a chance. And then you go to his place of business, and you—"

"I need you to stop and breathe, Haley," Reid commanded.

"You're upset, I understand, and I'm sorry for whatever has happened, but I assure you that all I did was ask Gavin a couple of questions. I was polite. I'm not entirely sure what he told you, but—"

"Why? What was so important that you couldn't talk with me first?"

"I was concerned. You've been exceedingly secretive about this man, called him a loner, and when I saw the background report—saw where he'd once worked and when, I had to know what was going on." Reid reached for her. She stepped away, out of his grasp. "And the reason I went to the hardware store was to find out when he was available, so we could keep the conversation private, until I learned the deal. But he insisted we talk then and there."

"What do you mean when you 'saw the background report'?" Haley asked, her voice now deadly calm. "Because if you mean what I think you mean, then I swear, Reid, I'll—"

"I mean what you think I mean, and I'm sorry for going that route. It was out of bounds." He held up his hands in a show of surrender. "But I worry about you, and as I said, you've been so secretive…that's unlike you, Haley."

"Uh-huh, and it's this sort of big-brother maneuver that propelled me to be secretive in the first place." She squeezed her eyes shut, pushed back the tears. She'd cry more later. Buckets more, she was sure. But not now, not if she could help it.

"Okay, I guess I can understand that," Reid said, watching her carefully. As if she might just blow up in front of him. "I apologize if my 'big-brother maneuvers' made you feel as if you couldn't confide in me. I never want that. You can always confide in me."

Why did he have to be so damn understanding? Didn't matter, she told herself, didn't matter in the slightest. She was *mad* at him. Needed to be mad in order to subdue the pain.

"You have no idea what you've done," she repeated. "None."

"Then tell me," Reid said. "Get it out."

"Gavin isn't used to people caring for him." She pushed the words out on top of another sob. "He grew up in foster care. His mother drank, couldn't take care of him because of the drinking. He bopped from one foster home to another. I was protecting what we were trying to build. Giving us time, giving him time, to believe in me. And what you did today?" she said, her voice raising with each syllable. "It didn't help."

Reid's complexion paled. "Oh, sweetheart. I had no idea. I was trying to protect you, that's all. Trying to keep you from getting hurt."

And that fired her up even more.

"Do you know what this amazing man is doing, Reid?" Angrily, she swiped at her cheeks as the tears began to fall harder. "He's bought this huge house, and he's saving every dollar for renovations so he can open a camp for foster kids, so he can give them something good. This is the man you were concerned about. This is the man I love. And now, I don't know if he'll give what's between us another shot." *Breathe,* she told herself. "And part of that rests on you."

Grief and sorrow weighted Reid's gaze. "What can I do? Whatever you want."

"Don't you get it? There's nothing to do now. Not one thing." She turned, to head up the stairs to her apartment, where she could be alone and cry to her heart's content, when she had another thought. Facing Reid again, she said, "Do you remember how you felt when Daisy left?"

"Yeah. Every day."

"Has it gotten any better over the years, or do you still miss her?"

Reid shut his eyes, expelled a sigh. "It isn't better, just

less…raw. And yes, I miss her. Always, I miss her. Always, I think about her."

"Wonderful. Good to know I'll never feel whole again." And then, all of her anger drained away, to be replaced by unrelenting sadness. She just about crumpled to her knees, her emotion—her despair—was that strong.

Her brother came to her, opened his arms. She stepped into them and sobbed as he held her, as he whispered apologies and promises that somehow, everything would be okay.

"I hate this," she whispered. "And I'm sorry for blowing up at you. Wasn't really your fault. Didn't help the situation in any way whatsoever, but not your fault."

Reid held her tighter, and she kept on crying. It seemed she'd never stop. Folks came in and out of the kitchen, but whenever anyone asked what was going on, he shooed them away. Even her parents. Even Dylan. Later, she knew, he'd explain the mess to them.

After a while, he convinced her to go upstairs, to her apartment, where he stayed and kept watch over her. Just as he had when she was a child and she'd wake from a nightmare.

Unfortunately, she knew with heartbreaking clarity that this was one nightmare that wouldn't disappear by morning.

Chapter Fourteen

The hammer smashed him cleanly on his thumb, which really was the perfect example of how the past week had gone. Gavin might not have a name for the depths of his misery, but it was bad. He couldn't sleep—couldn't even close his eyes without seeing Haley's tearstained face—couldn't eat and apparently he couldn't hammer a damn nail without injuring himself.

Cursing, not at all softly, he dropped the hammer on the floor and gave up. For the time being, his renovations had come to a screeching halt.

Upstairs, Gavin examined the damage to his thumb. Decided he'd live, and took a quick shower. Unsure of what to do, since he didn't work at the hardware store that day and didn't trust himself to do anything properly around the house, he meandered downstairs and plopped on the couch. Thought about Haley. Saw those tears of hers again.

Deciding he couldn't just sit around and think of Haley

or her tears, he stood up and went into the kitchen, where he thought he should probably try to eat even if he didn't feel hungry. Opened the cupboard…and darn if he didn't see Haley in his mind's eye, standing right where he was, telling him there was nothing to worry about and that he had plenty for lunch.

He missed her. He missed her voice, her touch, her laugh, the stubborn tilt of her chin.

Annoyed with himself, he grabbed a can of tomato soup from the cupboard. The last one he had from the three before, when she'd pushed her way into staying for that lunch. Cursing again, ignoring the god-awful pain in his thumb—which, as bad as it was, didn't come close to the pain in his heart—he opened the can.

Seemed no matter how hard he tried, he couldn't keep that woman out of his head for more than ten seconds at a time. She just lived there now, he guessed. Probably always would.

While the soup heated, he stalked the kitchen, unable to stand still. Decided he'd toast some bread to have with the soup, so he put a few slices of bread in the toaster. Stirred the soup. Stalked some more. Thought of Haley in this kitchen, moving around him as if she belonged here, as if she'd been in this room every friggin' day of her life.

Remembered how she reminded him of the sun.

The toast popped up in the toaster, the soup started to steam. He finished preparing his lunch, went to the table and started to eat. Thought about those silly questions of hers, and how she'd just keep at him until he answered. And then she'd ask him another. And on and on his brain went, moving from one memory to another, and every one of them centered on Haley.

Not the foster homes. Not his mother. Just Haley.

He had a thought, and knew it was a stupid one, but went to the cupboard to retrieve the peanut butter anyway. Had just finished spreading a glop of the stuff on his toast when he heard a vehicle rumble into his driveway. Looked outside, to see if he wanted to bother answering the door or just pretend he wasn't home. The identity of his visitors shocked him.

Worried him some, too.

Ignoring Haley's brothers, though, wasn't something he'd do, so Gavin went to the front door and stepped on the porch. Waited for them to reach him.

"Is Haley okay?" he asked, wanting to make that determination before anything else.

"Nah, wouldn't say she's okay. But she's breathing and I expect she'll get to okay eventually," Cole said, looking Gavin over in interest and curiosity. "We haven't been properly introduced. I'm Cole, and this here's Dylan. Believe you know Reid."

Reid walked up and held out his hand, which Gavin shook. "I owe you an apology," he said. "For snooping into your background as I did. Wasn't right, and I'm sorry I went that route."

"You were concerned about your sister. I understood that then, and I understand that now. That being said, I appreciate and accept the apology." Gavin leaned against the house, crossed his arms over his chest. Glanced from one Foster brother to the next. "Now, I'm guessing you're all here for a reason, though I can't quite figure out what that might be."

"The apology for one," Reid said. "We also wanted to drop off some materials. For the renovation Haley tells us you're in the middle of. She…she tore into me pretty good the day we talked, and let some of your plans slip in the midst of her…anger."

"Is that so?" Despite his misery, Gavin grinned at the image of Haley tearing into her brother. Would've been quite the sight. "I thank you for the thought, but I have no need of—"

"A lot of what we brought over are leftovers, from when I

overhauled my place," Cole said easily. "Some of the other…
Well, we'd like to help get this place in shape. See if we can
get that camp of yours started sooner rather than later."

"What you're planning on," Dylan said, entering the conversation, "is a real good thing. And it's something that all
of us Fosters—our parents included—would like to be a part
of. If you'll let us, however you'll let us. Whether that means
helping you raise money, with the actual manual labor, or
whatever. Just say the word and we'll do what we can."

"Did…Haley put you three up to this?" Had to be her.

"Oh, no," Reid said quickly, with a wry grin. "Pretty sure
she'd knock me into next year if she knew I was within spitting distance of you again. This is all us."

Gavin nodded, scratched his jaw. Tried to understand the
whys of this, just as he'd struggled to understand every last
step Haley had taken. "You Fosters are something else, aren't
you? I thought the barging in, the wanting to help, the impulsivity issues…thought that was all Haley, but I see she comes
by those traits naturally."

"We're a stubborn group," Dylan said with a smile that reminded Gavin of Haley's. Close, anyway. The same but without all the gloriousness of Haley's. "And we stand by those
we care about. Haley cares about you, so whether you like it
or not, that makes you one of us."

"Regardless of anything else," Cole added, shooting a
glance toward Reid and Dylan. "We'd like to be a part of
what you're doing here, and we hope you'll consider our sug-
gestion."

Gavin's initial response was to thank them again, decline
their generous offer and send them on their way. He didn't
need help. Never wanted to rely on anyone for anything, especially help. But he didn't say no right off, just let the idea
of it all simmer in his tired brain.

Maybe accepting help for something good, something that

would, in fact, help others, would be okay. And really, accepting help didn't mean he *required* help. All that meant was that he was smart to not go it alone when he didn't have to. There was logic there. Good, solid logic.

"I'll accept the materials and the help," he said. "But I'm not sure when I'll be ready to move forward again. Might be a few weeks. Might be longer. Can't say for sure."

All three Foster men let out a collective sigh, as if they'd been holding their breath in suspense of Gavin's answer. "We'll just unload what we have with us, then." Cole nodded toward the porch. "We'll leave it here, and you can do with it what you will. And you can always reach me at the sporting goods store. For whatever reason."

Gavin nodded, unsure of what else to say. If he could say anything else with the lump in his throat. Suddenly, without any warning at all, the world began to look a little different. A little more friendly. And that… Well, that made him think about all those possibilities he kept trying to ignore. Maybe—maybe he needed to reconsider those possibilities.

"I'll help with the unloading," he heard himself saying, "And…well, thank you. I'm unaccustomed to such…to folks being so friendly."

Dylan slapped him on his back and grinned. "Welcome. As I said, you're one of us now."

Twenty minutes later, the three men were gone and Gavin had a mess of stuff on his front porch. Some of which he knew he'd use. Some of the rest of it, he wasn't so sure. But he'd find a way to put all of it to good use, one way or another.

In the kitchen again, Gavin stared at his now-cold bowl of soup, the peanut butter toast, thought about Dylan's words—how Gavin was one of them now—and how neither Cole nor Reid had objected or tried to diminish the power of that statement.

Strangely, perhaps, this made him feel…positive. Gave him a good dose of courage.

He didn't have that sense of fear he so often had, of letting any one of them down. Of not being whatever they thought he should be. Gavin shook his head, wondering how this had happened, how he'd crossed a barrier he'd fought with most of his life.

Haley, of course. All of this had started with her. And in a rush of understanding, a comprehension he hadn't ever come close to attaining before, something hard and rocklike relaxed deep inside. There wasn't one damn thing wrong with him.

Which, of course, was the message Haley had tried to get across almost the entire time she'd known him. A message he couldn't hear, or refused to hear. Until now.

Gavin picked up the slice of toast he'd spread the peanut butter on. Stared at it for a minute, maybe two, folded the toast in half and dunked the sandwich in his soup. Took a large bite, just as Haley had done and…grimaced. Barely managed to swallow the horrible combination of flavors. And then… well, he tipped his head back and laughed.

Long and loud and…joyously.

Nope, he most definitely did not love peanut butter with tomato. He did, however, love the woman who'd inspired him to try. This, too, he let simmer for a moment, wanting to be absolutely sure before he did anything with this thought, this feeling. Before he took a step that he'd back away from. He wouldn't—couldn't—do that to Haley ever again.

"Well, dammit all," he muttered. The knowledge of what faced him, of the action he had to take, didn't sit well; it wasn't comfortable or easy. But he had to move forward. Had to dig out those demons from his closet and send them on their way. Forever, this time.

And since there was no sense in procrastinating, Gavin

went upstairs to retrieve the envelope his mother had given him. Tore open the flap, read her address and headed out.

Vanessa Daugherty opened the door to her studio apartment on the first knock, and her expression—the hope and surprise and happiness displayed there—slammed into Gavin with the force of a dozen lightning bolts. Despite everything else, he didn't want to hurt her. Didn't want her to run back to the bottle after being sober for nearly four years. And that meant he didn't want her hopes to grow too high before he understood where this conversation might lead.

If, in fact, it led anywhere at all.

So he started off by saying, "One conversation to begin with, that's all I'm promising. If—if you're able to handle the possibility of there never being another, I'd like to come in and talk with you. Otherwise, I'll be on my way."

"I'm only asking for one conversation," she said, without as much as a hint of hesitation or doubt. "So yes, Gavin, please come in."

He forced his legs to move and entered, looking around. The place was small, almost cramped, but clean and nicely— if generically—decorated. Okay, this helped. Knowing she hadn't been living in a dump while waiting on him helped.

Vanessa gestured toward a pair of chairs in front of a large window, saying, "Make yourself at home. Can I get you anything to drink? Eat?"

"Nope. Didn't come here to eat or drink." And that came out harsh. More so than he'd intended. Softening his voice, he said, "Thank you, though."

She led the way into the tiny living room and they each took a seat in one of the chairs. A sigh whispered from her, and she clutched her hands together in her lap. "I wasn't sure you would come. I hoped you would, but I wasn't sure."

"I wasn't sure, either. Until about thirty minutes ago."

Tongue-tied, he darted his eyes away from hers, unsure of who should talk, who should start. Unsure, too, if he felt the need to talk at all, or just wanted to listen. Deciding listening would be easier to begin with, he said, "This is your show, Mom. You came to Steamboat Springs for this conversation."

"Right. Of course." She twisted her fingers together nervously. "Now that the moment is here, I don't know where to begin. Other than to tell you again how sorry I am."

Now, dammit all, if this conversation turned out to be the same as all of the rest, then this was a waste of his time and energy. Hers, too. "What are you sorry for? Be clear."

"Everything, Gavin. I'm sorry for everything."

"That isn't clear." He stood. "I believe this was a mistake."

"No. This is not a mistake." She inhaled a breath. "I'm sorry I stopped being your mother when your father died. I'm…sorry you were making your own meals when you were five. I'm sorry for sending you to school wearing dirty clothes, because I couldn't handle basic chores."

Her voice dipped, weakened, and she curled her fingers into her palms, as if drawing strength. Her words, this action, propelled him to return to his chair. To sit down. To listen.

"I'm…I'm sorry for choosing booze to numb my grief, rather than helping you through yours. I'm sorry you ever had to see me, help me, when I was too drunk to even lift my head. Most of all, though, Gavin," she said in a rush of tear-soaked syllables, "I'm sorry…so very sorry you were stuck with a mother like me."

Gavin couldn't move. Couldn't do a damn thing but listen. This…yes, this was new. Something different from all of the times before. She hadn't hid the truth, hadn't chosen sterile terms to bury her apology in. Hadn't offered one excuse for her behavior.

And he believed her apologies. Believed her tears were centered in honesty, in the stark reality of what she'd done, who she'd been, for most of his entire life. The heavy weight of emotion crushed in, building behind in his throat, behind his eyes. He swallowed, hard, and blinked just as hard. He wasn't ready to cry in front of his mother.

More, he wasn't ready to let down that particular shield just yet. There was more to say, more to learn, more demons to slay.

"I need to know," he said, pushing the words out, forcing himself to go to this place he'd avoided for so long, "why you couldn't stay sober, those times you became sober. Need to know why I wasn't enough for you to want to be healthy."

Scraping tears from her cheeks with the palms of her hands, she looked him in the eyes. "Because I have a disease. Alcoholism is a disease. And until I could admit—"

"I know this. Know more about alcoholism than I care to, which is why I rarely drink," he interrupted. Never, in his life, did he want to travel the road his mother had. "I understand that while you were drinking, stopping would be—seem—impossible. But when you were sober, those times you managed to regain custody of me, why drink again then? I just don't get that."

"I… Yes, there were those times I found my way to sobriety, but they were never by choice." The flush of humiliation coated her cheeks. "I would become so ill that I was hospitalized, and when I became sober in those moments, I missed you so much. I so wanted to be with you, and I told myself I could do it. Except…I never could."

"Why?" he repeated for the gazillionth time.

"Not because of you. Not because I didn't love *you* enough." Vanessa closed her eyes and her tears grew in strength, in volume. "I never loved me enough to make the decision to get help. I had to make that choice in order to stay sober. Until I did, until that decision came from within me and I accepted the truth, the disease owned me."

Logically, Gavin understood her explanation. A person couldn't really accomplish much of anything if he or she wasn't doing so by choice. At least, not as successfully and, no, not long-term. Emotionally, he couldn't quite accept this as good enough.

In his mind, a child who needs his parent should be the trump card. *He* should have been his mother's trump card. *He* should have been enough for her to want to be healthy, to work at maintaining her sobriety, so she could take care of him.

But okay, she'd answered that question, and she had done so truthfully, without those platitudes he so despised. Whether he could come to terms with that truth remained to be seen. For now, he'd move on. Say the rest of what he'd fought with. "Do you have any idea how miserable most of those foster homes were?"

"No," she said quietly. "But I can guess. And the fact you grew up in such a way, due to my inabilities, my illness, haunts me. I can't explain how much I hate what I've done to you."

Unable to sit any longer, Gavin stood and paced the small room. "There was a couple who wanted to adopt me, but couldn't. Because of you, because you were once again insisting you could stay healthy and care for me. So...the state didn't allow the adoption. And do you remember how long I was with you that time? Three months. Only three months."

"I know all of this, Gavin. I know...and—"

"No, you don't know! This was a good family. I loved them, they loved me. I could have had a normal life...but you wouldn't let that happen, you wouldn't let me go so I could have something better. Better than you were able to give. To be."

"This won't, and shouldn't, matter now, but if I could redo that decision, I would let you go. For all the reasons you just said." Cradling her face in her hands, she breathed in and steadied herself. After a moment, she sat up straight, looked at him. And he saw a woman stripped of her defenses. A woman who was acutely aware of herself, of the damage she'd caused. "You deserved far better. I will always regret my actions in this regard. Always."

Well, she was wrong. This sentiment, along with the honesty he heard in her voice, did matter. Nope, the past couldn't be changed...but knowing his mother understood what she had done to him, even if she couldn't change any of it, mattered. A hell of a lot.

"Okay. That means something. Don't think it doesn't," he said, battling a tide of emotion he wasn't sure he'd be able to hold back much longer. He was done for now. Had heard enough for now. "Thank you for being truthful. For answering my questions."

His mother's face was blotchy. Her body still trembled. And her eyes were filled with a deep, unrelenting sadness. He saw something else, though. He saw her love for him.

"Thank you," she said, "for giving me the opportunity."

"I... You're welcome," he said somewhat gruffly. "Did you get that job at the Beanery?"

"I did. I start next week."

Well, then. They'd have more time to hash out their history, more time to see if they could have a fresh start, not just in Steamboat Springs, but with each other. If they could, if that were possible, and if they could work toward a healthier relationship, he would...welcome it.

"I'm glad," he said, admitting the truth. If she could put herself out there for him, for his regard, then he guessed he could do the same for her. For them.

"Are you?" She blinked, emotion welled in her eyes, but she kept the tears at bay. "I'll see you again? Talk with you again?"

He gave a short nod. "We'll have to do this slowly, but yes, we'll see each other again."

And then, Gavin did something he hadn't done in over a decade. Maybe longer. He walked to his mother, grasped her hand and pulled her up, and hugged her. Held her tight for a minute. So she would know, even if he couldn't yet verbalize the emotion, that he still loved her.

When they separated, sadness still clung to her expression. Hope was there, as well. Now, though, he didn't see that hope as futile. He saw that hope as…a possibility. For the chance at them becoming a real family someday.

After he left, he sat in his truck, allowing himself a few minutes to begin processing the time he'd just spent with his mother. No. The pain of his past hadn't evaporated with one honest conversation, but the ache felt different. Lighter. Easier to carry.

Good enough. More than he'd expected.

What had disappeared, though, was the hold his past had on today. On tomorrow. On a future with Haley. Of course, he'd have to work darn hard to convince her to forgive him. To give him one more—one final—chance. If she did, he'd never need another.

Because now, he believed.

Chapter Fifteen

"Okay, you bozos. Where are you taking me in such a rush?" Haley asked her brothers—all three of them—from the front seat of Reid's SUV. They'd shown up at her apartment thirty minutes ago at a ridiculously early hour and had awakened her quickly. Insisted she get dressed. And then, insisted she'd moped long enough and that it was time to leave her apartment.

She'd pointed out that she left her apartment every day, when she walked downstairs to do her job. Funnily enough, they didn't think that counted. And while they hadn't seen the extent of her moping just yet—not even close—she didn't have the heart to argue with them.

Simply speaking, her brothers had taken care of her pretty much nonstop since that crushing afternoon with Gavin. They'd brought her chocolates—lots of chocolates. They'd made her laugh. They'd even watched one sappy romantic comedy after another with her, silently handing her tissues as she cried. And when her tears turned to anger, they'd handled that, too.

Yes, her brothers had been there for her. So if they believed she needed a morning out, she'd give them a morning out. Even if she'd rather eat chocolate and cry.

"You can't just wake a person up and not tell them where you're taking them," she said, trying again. "Not only is that unfair, but it's weird."

"It's a surprise," Dylan said from the backseat. "No more questions."

"I'm no longer a huge fan of surprises," she retorted.

"Ah. I think you'll like this one," Reid said from the driver's seat. "Hope so, anyway."

She feigned an exasperated sigh, and stared out the window at the darkness. The sky held the slightest, barely there glow. A promise that the sun would rise soon to chase away the shadows of the night. Somehow, this promise relaxed her. Dug in deep and pulled out a strand of hope that maybe this day, unlike each day from the past week, would be different.

Each of those days had been filled with a sickening surety that she would never feel true happiness again. Oh, she expected she'd find her balance at some point, would be able to smile and laugh and carry on. But she'd been wrong before, when she'd thought that loving a man who didn't love her for the rest of her life would be the worst possible outcome of her relationship with Gavin. That nothing else could possibly compare with such a pain.

This—loving Gavin and believing he loved her, even if he hadn't said the words—was far worse. Because whatever kept him from sharing his love, from accepting her love, resulted in nothing more than a huge, fat waste, in every way that she could see. Together, they could fight any battle and win. Together, they could be…everything.

Unfortunately, unless he figured that out, this current reality they were stuck in wouldn't change. And that, in her opinion, made this far worse than if she believed he just didn't love her.

She sighed again, stared at the road as they drove. It didn't take long to reach their destination, and when her vision locked on the one and only sign that declared where they were, she frowned. What in heaven's name were her brothers thinking?

"Really, guys?" she asked, bewildered. "You woke me up at the freaking crack of dawn to take me on a hot-air balloon ride? Who had this idea?"

"We're not taking you on a hot-air balloon ride," Cole said, also from the backseat. "Consider us your chauffeurs. And maybe your chaperones, if you're unhappy with the plan, once you're told what that plan is. If everything really goes south, we might even become—"

"Talking too much," Dylan said in a singsong voice. "Way too much."

"Eh. We're here. She's about three minutes from knowing, anyway."

Reid parked the SUV, unhooked his seat belt and faced her. "We're going to wait right here, so if you're unhappy for any reason, all you have to do is come back."

"What's going on?" Haley said in a half whisper, believing she knew what might be happening, but too afraid to trust those instincts. In case she was wrong. "Just tell me."

"Huh-uh. We can't. We made a promise," Reid said just as softly. "But listen, all of this is for you, and I…we just want you to be happy. That's all we've ever wanted for you."

"I know this, Reid." She looked over her shoulder at Cole and Dylan. "I know."

"Good. Okay, so all you have to do is get out of the car and walk straight toward that building." Reid leaned over and kissed her forehead. "And we'll be here for a while."

With shaking hands and a jittery pulse, she unhooked her seat belt. "Is it Gavin?" she asked, putting her belief into words. "You have to tell me. If I walk out there and he isn't waiting for me, my heart will break all over again. And I don't know if I can handle that."

"Sweetheart," Reid said calmly. "Go. Just go and find out for yourself."

So she did, but her entire body trembled as she exited the vehicle, as she walked through the darkness toward the building. God. She so wanted to see Gavin. So wanted him to have decided—without her typical brand of interference—that he wanted to be with her. But she was, in all ways, very much afraid that she'd be let down. That something else was happening here.

She arrived at the building, but the door was locked. Pivoting on her heel to look around, she didn't see anyone. Her heart thumped even harder, and her legs grew more jellylike. In front of the building was a bench, so she went there and sat down. Breathed.

And tried not to hope too hard.

Then, seemingly from nowhere, there he was. *Gavin.* The missing piece of her soul. He rounded the side of the building from the back and sat down next to her. At first, he didn't speak. She didn't, either. Just soaked in his presence, the solid, real feel of him beside her, and despite her attempts, her hope started to grow.

"Haley," he said after a few seconds, "I've missed you."

"I've missed you, too," she admitted. "But I don't know what's going on here, and my brothers wouldn't tell me. And, Gavin? You need to know I'm good and peeved with you."

"I'm glad your brothers didn't say anything, and, Haley, you have the right to be peeved." He ran his hand over his jaw, still clean-shaven, and pushed out a short breath. "I don't deserve anything from you, but I'm hoping you'll give me the opportunity to say a few words."

"I'll listen," she said. Of course she'd listen. Would never forgive herself if she didn't. Even so, she tried to remind herself that this—as positive as everything appeared—might not be what she was thinking. "But after I listen, I get to talk, too."

"I would expect as much," he said with a fair bit of humor. Nervousness, too. She heard both, clear as day. "I...well, I still don't rightly know if you can understand, but I know you'll try. And I figure I owe you an explanation. A real, true, honest explanation."

"Yes, you do." Bam, bam, bam went her heart.

"Growing up as I did taught me a whole bunch of lessons I'm only now realizing aren't completely accurate." He stopped, as if to gather his thoughts. Then, "I'm not specifically talking about the foster homes, though those are a part of the whole. My mother is also there, in the mix, and her inability to take care of herself. To take care of me when I was a child."

"I can't imagine how your life was, Gavin. But I know it wasn't easy."

"Nope, none of anything to do with my mother was ever easy. There's a lot there I wouldn't mind sharing with you, if we get to the point that sharing makes sense, but for now... well, what I need to say right now, is that due to my experiences, to these lessons I learned, I put up all of these barriers. Shields, I guess. And they got me through, Haley."

"I understand that well enough." And she did, had actually understood this aspect of Gavin's personality for a while. "You learned to protect yourself the only way you could, based on what was happening around you. That makes total sense."

His body relaxed slightly. "Exactly. Until you came along

and, one by one, shattered every damn barrier I had in place. I tried to rebuild them. I tried to pretend I could be with you without letting you all the way in, because that felt safer. That felt doable."

"But that won't work in a real relationship," she said softly. Did he understand that now, or was this only an apology and an explanation? She didn't know. Hadn't yet figured that out. "In any relationship—good ones, at least—you have to let the other person in."

"I know. When I couldn't, I…decided you'd be better off with someone who could."

She shook her head, a bit of her anger surfacing. "Oh, I see. You decided what I needed, what would be best for me, without so much as saying a word to me?"

"Well…yes."

"You silly, silly man." Haley closed her eyes, counted to three. "I don't want to be with anyone else. And you could walk away now and never look back, and even then, I doubt my decision in this matter would ever change."

His breath hitched. "That's because you're stubborn."

"Hmm. Yes. Also because I know myself, know what I want."

"And impulsive," he said as if she hadn't spoken. "Impatient. Nosy, too."

Narrowing her eyes, she said, "Well, you're gruff and distant and…and…blind as a freaking bat in the middle of the afternoon. Why, I had to shove myself in front of you in order for you to even see me. And I had to do this over and over and over."

Gavin laughed that wonderful laugh of his, and the sound of it unhinged a few of the knots in her stomach. "Yup. I'd say those are accurate statements. But you don't know how to take no for an answer, and you enjoy barging in on folks as if it's the highlight of your life, and you…you like peanut butter toast and tomato soup. Together!"

He shuddered as he made that last comment, and while she had no clue what her odd food preferences had to do with this conversation, that thready strand of hope grew larger. "You're impulsive, too," she said, her voice now quiet. "Otherwise, I wouldn't be here now."

"Nope, I don't expect you would be." Suddenly, he stood and held his hand out toward her. "It'll be light soon, and I'd very much like to go on a hot-air balloon ride with you," he said. "The balloon is ready to go. They're just waiting on us."

"I've never been in a hot-air balloon."

"I've heard it's quite the sight. And I'd like to do this with you."

She didn't know what his plan was, but decided the only way to find out was to agree. Putting her hand in his, she said, "Well, then. Let's go on a hot-air balloon ride. Even if it's early enough to…fish."

Another laugh. "Trust me. This will be worth the early-morning hour. And you won't have to touch a worm."

They walked together to the field behind the building, to the balloon that was ready and waiting to go. Once they stepped inside the basket, the balloon's weight was balanced, and then, one by one, the ropes were unsecured. And in almost no time at all, they were flying.

Gavin stood directly behind her, with his hands on her waist and his jaw resting on the top of her head. His voice, that deep, husky tenor of his, whispered, "Close your eyes."

"Why?"

"Must you argue about everything?" he asked. "Just close your eyes. Please."

"Okay. I'll close my eyes." Haley breathed in the morning air, did as Gavin asked and shut her eyes, and let the sensation of drifting weightless in the air overtake her.

And this, the sensation and being so close to Gavin, her hope that was slowly and surely turning into belief, reconnected some of the pieces inside that had been broken and shattered. Brought her closer to feeling whole—real—again. But she wasn't all the way there. Couldn't get all the way there until, unless, Gavin said the words she craved to hear.

As they floated, he wrapped his arms more fully around her, gently tugged her backward so she was leaning against him, against his strength. "I'm sorry," he said. "Sorry for not trusting you enough to let you all the way in. I wasn't ready, Haley."

"Trust isn't all that easy to give," she said. "Even without the battles you've had."

"Still, you should know I'm sorry."

"I'm sorry, too. For the barging in and the not listening." Resting her head against his chest, she sighed. The apology needed to be said, and she meant it, but she knew full well that she'd do the same today. For him. For them. "For tricking you to go on the camping trip."

"I don't want you to apologize for those actions. If you hadn't...been open to the possibilities, seen something that I couldn't see... Well, I think that would be sad."

Yes, sad. More than that. The thought was...devastating.

With her eyes still closed, she reveled in the moment. In her hopes and dreams. In every last thing she believed could exist with this man...with *only* this man. A minute or so passed in easy silence and pure anticipation.

"Are your eyes still closed?" he asked.

"Yes," she said, her heart dancing in her chest.

"Good. I'm going to count to three, and then I'd like you to open your eyes. Okay?"

"Okay."

"One...two...three." His chest moved with a deep breath. "Open your eyes."

She opened her eyes and gasped—in wonder, in exhilaration—at the sight before her, at a sunrise seen from the vantage point of a hot-air balloon. Rays of light, from white to gold to a warm coppery red, stretched and shimmied through the puffy clouds, making them—and the sky itself—appear almost iridescent. Beautiful. Shimmery and majestic. Awe-inspiring.

Everywhere she looked, all she saw was…magic.

"This is amazing. So beautiful," she said breathlessly. "Look, Gavin. It's like we're in an entirely different world. I've never… Didn't know a sunrise could look like this."

"This is what I wanted you to see. Because, to me," he said, his mouth near her ear, his breath warm on her skin, "this is you. To me, you are the sun in all its life-affirming glory."

"Gavin," she whispered, caught up in the moment, in his words, in the way he viewed her. In the feel of his arms, and the solidity of his body. "How can you see me like this? I'm just a person and this…this is magic. This is—"

"Who you are to me." Shifting his hands to her shoulders, he twisted her around to face him. And in his eyes, she saw the world. *Her* world. "It took me a while to figure this out, but I love you, Haley Foster. With all of who I am today and all of who I'll be tomorrow. And I'd hoped—I'm standing here hoping now—that you'll give me one more chance."

Well, duh. Of course she would. How could she say no to this man? First, though, "You hurt me, and I can't feel that way again with you, the loss of you. So if you want this chance, then I need you to stay. To try. To not give up." She touched his cheek. "I need you to believe."

Bringing his hand to hers, he twisted their fingers together. His gaze held hers, steadily. Surely. "I do and I will. I promise you I will never willingly walk away again."

"Oh, thank God," she said, hearing his love, the truth and,

most of all, the belief. *His* belief. "I love you, too, Gavin. So yes, another chance. For both of us."

"We'll never need another. I can promise you that, as well." He paused, swallowed. "You're the sun, Haley. My sun, and I can't live without you, can't live in darkness any longer."

"Kiss me," she whispered. "Before I start crying."

Slowly, gently, he lowered his mouth to hers. The second their lips touched, heat curled and spread through her body, inch by inch, limb by limb. This kiss was like the others, in its intensity and passion. In the way her heart sped and her bones weakened. Also, though, this kiss held something different the others hadn't. The promise of a future...*their* future, made up of who they were. Her family. His past. *Their* dreams, goals and hopes.

Somehow, she knew, all of this would combine to form the road they would travel on, hand in hand, toward a future meant only for them.

Yes, together they could be—would be—everything.

Epilogue

Gavin stretched and rolled, looking for Haley. Her side of the bed was empty, and his heart lurched for just a second before returning to its normal rhythm. In the months that had passed since their hot-air balloon ride, many, many changes had taken place. He and his mother were talking more regularly, had found a place of…comfort, he supposed.

Their relationship would continue to grow, would continue to strengthen. Day by day, with each conversation, his resentments were fading into the background. Day by day, the possibilities of life had become joyous and exciting, rather than limiting and frightening. And, day by day, his love for Haley deepened and became even more intrinsic to who he was.

Every now and again, there'd be a moment, like just now when he'd seen Haley's empty side of the bed, and he'd have a second where his old fear would return. Each time this happened, though, the fear disappeared more quickly than the time before. He believed that soon enough, the negative emotion would be gone for good.

Standing, he looked outside, saw the big, white puffy flakes dropping from the sky and grinned. Today was Christmas. His very first Christmas with Haley, and he had a special gift for her. One in which he hoped she'd understand what giving her this particular gift signified. For him. To their future, down the road a ways.

Smiling, he took the stairs, sure now that she was waiting for him in the living room, in front of the fireplace she adored, beyond excited at giving him whatever surprises she'd chosen. Lord, that woman enjoyed surprising him. He enjoyed surprising her, as well.

At the foot of the stairs, he stopped and listened to the somewhat strange, muffled sounds emanating from the living room. Curious, he stepped to the edge of the room and stopped again. Stared. Shook his head and turned around before Haley saw him in order to grab his digital camera. This, without a doubt, needed to be photographed.

With his camera in hand, he returned to the living room, this time walking all the way in. Snapped a couple of shots before Haley realized he was there.

The woman he loved was half under the damn tree. One hand on a present and the other on the head of the scruffiest puppy he'd ever laid eyes on. And this woman, this feisty, impulsive woman, was anxiously trying to get that poor dog to chew open the gift she held.

Unfortunately, the pup was far more interested in chewing on a hunk of Haley's hair than it was in tearing open wrapping paper. Still, warmth spread and slid throughout his body, from the bottom of his feet to the top of his head. How in the hell had he gotten this lucky?

"Haley," he said, making himself known, swallowing the

laughter ready to barrel out of his chest. "You can't force that dog to do something that dog doesn't want to do."

His voice startled her enough that she jumped, which sent the pup into a barking spin, tugging and pulling at Haley's hair. "You're not supposed to be up yet," Haley said, trying to separate her hair from the dog's mouth and failing miserably. "I'm not ready!"

"Well now, I can see what you're trying to do here, and I appreciate the thought, but there isn't any way that pup is going to do what you want."

"Oh, she will, too. I just haven't quite convinced her yet," Haley said, her voice filled with determination. "So…go back upstairs. Give me ten minutes. Fifteen tops!"

"Nope, it's Christmas morning, and honestly—"

That was all that came out of his mouth before bedlam set in. The pup, in her excitement to play with Haley, tugged a little too hard, and Haley, in her desire to be free of the pup's mouth, yanked her entire body backward a little too fast. The result of which was the tree falling straight over and landing on the ground, ornaments flying and the dog getting the hell out of Dodge…fast.

"Well, hell," she hollered out, obviously—and thankfully—unhurt. "This was not what was supposed to happen." Branches on the tree rustled, causing several more ornaments to come loose and roll on the hardwood floor. "Um. Gavin? I actually think I'm stuck."

"You think?" he asked, already moving toward her. Well. Wait. One more picture first, just for the sake of posterity. Once that was done, he lifted the tree and waited for Haley to crawl out from beneath. She did, sweeping her hair away from her face, pine needles all over her, and cursed. Loudly. Colorfully. And he grinned all the more.

God, he loved this woman.

She shoved her hands on her hips and turned in a circle,

either looking at the mess or for the dog. "I ruined Christmas," she half wailed. "And this was supposed to be the perfect morning. I wanted you to... I wanted to remind you of Russ and Elaine, of that Christmas, and now, we have a mess—which, I suppose, was part of my goal—and I don't see that dog."

He drew her into his arms, kissed her soundly. "I love you."

"I love you, too, but that doesn't change the fact that I—"

"Tried to do something wonderful," he said in no uncertain terms. "And really, other than the tree on the floor, this is pretty close to how I remember that morning."

Her eyes lit up. "Really?"

"Really." Well, no, but that was fine. The emotion was the same. And to his way of thinking, that was all that mattered. And then, because he'd held it back for so long, he laughed. "I have to say, though, that finding you under the tree trying to coerce that dog was about the funniest sight I've been witness to in a long, long while."

"I just wanted to make this morning special for you," she said, picking pine needles out of her hair. "And I thought it would be nice to have a dog here, for when the camp opens. Kids love dogs, so... I don't know, maybe I should've thought this one through more."

"Nope. You absolutely shouldn't have. I love that you did this. Though," he said, giving the room another appraisal, "we should probably pick up. Before your family arrives."

The entire Foster clan had become involved in readying the house and the property, and as of now, everything was almost in order. If not by summer, then in no more than another year, the camp would officially open. And he couldn't have done any of this as well or as quickly without the support, the help, of Haley's family.

Together, he and Haley made quick work of cleaning and redecorating the tree. Then, over cups of coffee and cinnamon rolls from the Beanery, they opened their gifts to each other. It seemed to take forever, but finally she reached for the gift he'd thought long and hard over.

As she had with every other present, she shook the box before tearing into the paper. He held his breath, waiting, wondering if she'd see what he'd tried to do, tried to show her.

Lifting the lid, her almost-green eyes widened. Emotion sifted in, softening her features and coating her cheeks in that seductive, rosy glow. "This…is perfect," she said in a hush. "Absolutely, positively perfect. How…you remembered. I can't believe you remembered."

"Of course I remembered," he said. "Come here, let me help you with that."

Eyes shiny with unshed tears—happy tears, he knew— she nodded, scooted over and held out the necklace he'd purchased. "Thank you, Gavin."

His heart thumped as he accepted the necklace, as he considered how he wanted to say the words he needed for her to hear. The pendant—a sprig of mistletoe—hung from a relatively long chain, which he held above her head. His own emotion, strong and sure, swept over him.

Meeting her gaze with his, he said, "Someday, down the road a ways, we'll have a little girl. Or maybe a boy. But I want our child to see us the way you saw your parents when you were ten, on Christmas Eve. I want our children to feel secure and loved and—" he stopped, pulled in air, steadied his voice "—to always know what being a part of a real family feels like."

"Oh. Just…oh." One tear and then two dripped out of her beautiful eyes. Then he kissed her, this woman he loved. This woman he would always love.

Sometimes, Gavin thought as he pulled Haley closer to him, as he deepened their kiss, a man has to know when to surrender. More important, perhaps, a man has to be able to recognize the right person he should surrender to.

And he was damn glad he'd somehow managed to do both.

* * * * *

COMING NEXT MONTH
from Harlequin® Special Edition®
AVAILABLE AUGUST 20, 2013

#2281 THE MAVERICK & THE MANHATTANITE
Montana Mavericks: Rust Creek Cowboys
Leanne Banks
When Sheriff Gage Christensen meets energetic Lissa Roarke, a volunteer helping with Rust Creek's flood restoration efforts, he soon finds he's got more than rebuilding the town on his mind.

#2282 THE ONE WHO CHANGED EVERYTHING
The Cherry Sisters
Lilian Darcy
Daisy Cherry annoys her sister Lee when she hires Lee's ex-fiancé, Tucker, for a landscaping project. Little does Daisy know there's more than old enmity brewing between her and Tucker....

#2283 A VERY SPECIAL DELIVERY
Those Engaging Garretts!
Brenda Harlen
Lukas Garrett miraculously delivers Julie Marlowe's son during a blizzard. Though Lukas bonds with Julie and newborn, Caden, can the couple overcome Julie's tragic past to create a bright new future?

#2284 LOST AND FOUND FATHER
Family Renewal
Sheri WhiteFeather
In high school, Ryan Nash abandoned his pregnant girlfriend, Victoria. When Victoria contacts her now-adult daughter and takes her to meet Ryan, sparks fly—and a family is born.

#2285 THE BONUS MOM
Jennifer Greene
While on a hike, botanist Rosemary MacKinnon finds more than she bargained for—handsome widower Whit and his twin daughters. The outdoorsy duo forms a bond, but can family spring anew from emotional ashes?

#2286 DOCTOR, SOLDIER, DADDY
The Doctors MacDowell
Caro Carson
When army doc Jamie MacDowell marries orderly Kendry Harrison, he just wants a mother for his newborn son. But can he overcome his past to recognize love in the present?

You can find more information on upcoming Harlequin®
titles, free excerpts and more at www.Harlequin.com.

HSECNM0813

REQUEST YOUR FREE BOOKS!
2 FREE NOVELS PLUS 2 FREE GIFTS!

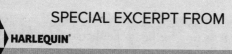
***

"I'm so excited I can't stand it," she admitted. "We can finally start getting something done."

Her enthusiasm burrowed inside him. He smiled. "Yeah, that's good. And we all appreciate it."

"Thanks," she said. "I'm going to make an early night of it, so I'll be ready to greet the volunteers tomorrow. Thank you for getting me some wheels."

"My pleasure," Gage said. "But no—"

"Driving in the snow," she finished for him. "That ditch was no fun for me, either."

"It's dark. You want me to walk you back to the rooming house?" He offered because he wanted to extend his time with her.

"I think I'll be okay," she said. "Rust Creek isn't the most crime-ridden place in the world. But thank you for your chivalry."

Gage gave a rough chuckle. "No one's ever accused me of being chivalrous."

"Well, maybe they haven't been watching closely enough."

Gage felt his gut take a hard dip at her statement. He knew

that Lissa was struggling with her visit to Rust Creek and he hadn't made it as easy for her as he should have. There was some kind of electricity or something between them that he couldn't quite name. Just looking at her did something to him.

"I'll take that as a compliment. Call me if you need me," he said.

"Thank you," she said. "Good night."

"Good night," he said, and wished she was going home with him to his temporary trailer to keep him warm. Crazy, he told himself. All wrong. She was Manhattan. He was Montana. Big difference. The twain would never meet. Right?

***

We hope you enjoyed this sneak peek from
USA TODAY *bestselling author Leanne Banks's new*
Harlequin Special Edition book,
THE MAVERICK & THE MANHATTANITE,
the next installment in
MONTANA MAVERICKS: RUST CREEK COWBOYS,
the brand-new six-book continuity launched in July 2013!

SADDLE UP AND READ 'EM!

Looking for another great Western read? Check out these September reads from HOME & FAMILY category!

CALLAHAN COWBOY TRIPLETS by Tina Leonard
Callahan Cowboys
Harlequin American Romance

HAVING THE COWBOY'S BABY by Trish Milburn
Blue Falls, Texas
Harlequin American Romance

HOME TO WYOMING by Rebecca Winters
Daddy Dude Ranch
Harlequin American Romance

*Look for these great Western reads and more
available wherever books are sold or visit*
www.Harlequin.com/Westerns

HARLEQUIN®

SPECIAL EDITION

Life, Love and Family

Be sure to check out the first book in this year's
FAMILY RENEWAL miniseries
by bestselling author Sheri WhiteFeather.

During high school, Ryan Nash dated Victoria Allen.
When Victoria got pregnant, they turned to adoption.
However, when Ryan failed to show up for their
daughter's birth, Victoria never spoke to him again.
Fast-forward eighteen years later and both Victoria
and her daughter, Kaley, have set out on a search for
each other. A slow and steady bond builds between
them, but when Kaley wants to meet her birth
father, will this family find their happily-ever-after?

*Look for LOST AND FOUND FATHER next month
from Harlequin® Special Edition® wherever books
and ebooks are sold!*

HSE65766

HARLEQUIN®

A *Romance* FOR EVERY MOOD™

Love the Harlequin book you just read?

Your opinion matters.

Review this book on your favorite book site, review site, blog or your own social media properties and share your opinion with other readers!